Reckless

Adventures in Love Series

Rushed

Risky

Reckless

Alfha Law Series (written as C.A Rose)

Justified

Liability

Stand-Alone Novels

Love at the Bluebird

The Wrong/Right Man

Finders Keepers (written as C.A Rose)

To Have to Hold to Keep Series

Trapping Her

Taking Her (coming soon)

Stalking Her (coming soon)

Reckless

Adventures in Love

AURORA ROSE REYNOLDS

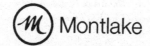

Montlake

Published by Montlake, Seattle

www.apub.com

Amazon, the Amazon logo, and Montlake are trademarks of Amazon.com, Inc., or its affiliates.

ISBN-13: 9781542034852 (paperback)
ISBN-13: 9781542034845 (digital)

Cover design by Letitia Hasser
Cover photography by Regina Wamba of ReginaWamba.com
Cover image: © Pavel Matejka / EyeEm / Getty

Printed in the United States of America

Reckless

Chapter 1

JADE

With my gaze trained on the road ahead of me, I focus on the yellow lines that are barely visible through the thick snow falling steadily from the dark sky above.

"Stupid," I mumble to myself, knowing for sure that if I hadn't stopped to eat and wander around a large trading post packed to the brim with stuff to look at, I most likely wouldn't be driving through this mess right now.

Then again, I knew the risk I was taking leaving Oregon for Montana today, with a blizzard forecast all over the news. A storm that not only my dad but Cybil, my best friend, and her husband, Tanner, warned me about over and over again.

Not that I listened to any of them. I mean, why would I do something ridiculous like take sound advice from people I trust? I never do that, which is not only why I'm in the middle of a snowstorm I have no business driving in but also why my bookstore closed and my life went tits up.

Okay, so my business didn't close because I didn't take the advice of others; that all happened because Mag McGregor decided that it was absolutely unholy for a store in her town to sell sex toys and books with sex in them. Then she went about making it uncomfortable for anyone to shop in my store even if they were just there to purchase a good ol' self-help book.

How the woman found out about the hidden room in the back of my bookstore, where the walls were covered in sex toys I sold, is still anyone's guess, but I'd bet my last dollar she would be a whole lot happier if she had taken the time to find herself a special toy and then use it every once in a while.

All that said, my life did go tits up because I didn't take advice. Like the advice my best friend tried to give me about not dating Carl when I had dated him in the past and he'd cheated on me. Or the advice my mom gave me about not letting Carl borrow money to help him start up a painting business. If I had listened to either of them, I might not be jobless, homeless, manless, broke as a joke, and driving in the middle of a blizzard right now.

Sighing, I ease my foot off the gas when I see a semi come around a bend in the road ahead of me, its bright headlights making it even more difficult to see even a few feet in front of me through the snow. I hold my breath and the steering wheel a little tighter as it passes, my tires seeming to have a hard time keeping a grip on the road as I head up a hill.

When I reach the top, I let out the breath I've been holding and wonder if I should just find somewhere to pull over and park for the night. Even with the GPS telling me that I will be at Cybil and Tanner's house in just over an hour, I'm not sure that my little car will make it with the roads getting worse by the second.

Like my best friend knows I'm thinking about her, my cell phone ringing cuts off the song currently playing, and I press the button on the steering wheel to answer. "Hey," I chirp, hoping not to sound as anxious as I feel at the moment.

"How far away are you?" she asks, sounding worried, then adds: "The roads are getting bad here."

"About an hour. The roads are getting bad here too." I gasp when the back of my car swings to the left, then the right.

"What happened? Are you okay?"

"I'm fine. The snow is just starting to really stick to the road." I hold the steering wheel tighter and wish I had taken my dad's advice and put on my snow tires.

"Pull over. I'm coming to get you," she says, and I start to tell her that she's not, but Tanner beats me to the punch when I hear him tell her that she is not driving in the storm right before the phone is shuffled. Knowing Cybil, I'm sure she's trying to keep me from hearing them argue, but I still hear her tell him that she is and him tell her she's not, before the sound is cut off almost completely. Then I hear a smack of lips, and she comes back on the line. "So." She clears her throat, sounding a little dazed, which makes me smile. "Tanner says that he's going to call Maverick—his truck will be able to make it to wherever you are."

"Maverick?"

"Tanner's best friend—you know him." I do know him, or kind of—we've been around each other on a few occasions but never for more than a couple of hours at a time. I have always considered myself someone who is really good at reading people, but he's unreadable. The only things I really know about him are that he's been best friends with Tanner, my best friend's husband, since they were in the military together, he's seriously attractive, and he has an easy smile. And from what Cybil says, he has a way with my niece, Claire, Cybil and Tanner's daughter.

"I'll be fine. If the road gets too bad, I'll find a place to park until the snowplows and salt trucks come out."

"Jade, please don't be difficult right now. I know that you can handle yourself in most situations, but we're talking about you driving in the middle of a blizzard."

"Fine," I agree with a huff, because even if I know she's right, I don't like giving in. "I'll get off on the next exit and find someplace to stay for the night."

"Is there an exit coming up?" she asks, and just then a green sign appears in the distance.

"Yes, or I think so—there is a sign coming up."

"Perfect." She sounds relieved, but I'm not when the sign gets closer and I see that it's one for a rest area that lets me know that there will not be another exit for twenty more miles.

"What does the sign say?"

"Umm, it's for a rest area. I'm going to pull in there and park."

"What is the exit number?"

"Cybil, please, I don't feel comfortable with Tanner calling his friend to come rescue me."

"That's too bad, because I don't feel comfortable with you putting your life at risk or sleeping in your car overnight at some rest stop in the middle of a snowstorm," she snaps.

"All right, calm down." I silently curse my stupid luck of late and rattle off the exit number, which she immediately relays to Tanner, who I'm guessing is on the phone with Maverick.

"Okay, Mav knows where you are, and he said he will be there shortly."

"Sounds great," I lie as I exit the highway, finding a half dozen semis and a few cars parked along the entryway into the lot.

"How's Pebbles doing?" she asks as I pull into a parking spot and put my car in park. I look over at my companion, who has been asleep in his dog bed, which is buckled into the front seat, since we left the trading post.

"He's passed out." I reach over and run my fingers over the top of Pebbles's head, and he barely opens his eyes to look at me, but his little tail does start to wag. "Since we're here, I'm going to see if I can get him to go potty."

"Okay, just let me know when you get back in the car after."

"Sure, Mom," I say sarcastically and listen to her laugh, which makes me smile, then say a quick goodbye with a promise to see her soon. After we hang up, it takes me a minute to get Pebbles in his sweater and to put on my jacket, both of which were too hot to wear in the car with the heat blowing.

Once I have my beanie on and Pebbles's leash attached to his collar, I push open the door to my car and regret the decision almost immediately. Even with my winter coat, boots, and hat, the cold air steals my breath, freezing me from the inside out, while Pebbles, who is against my chest, shivers from head to tail.

With purpose in my step, I head for the sidewalk and go past a large building lit up with golden, warm light toward the area for dogs. When I reach the spot to let Pebbles loose, I hate myself a little. Pebbles was the runt of his litter and weighs about eight pounds soaking wet. He's tiny, my baby, the only guy besides my dad who's stuck around.

I kick away the layer of snow that has collected on the grass and kiss his nose before I set him down, telling him, "Potty." Something he doesn't hesitate to do, knowing that the faster he goes, the faster I will pick him back up and get him out of the cold.

Once I have him up and in my arms, I walk with my head ducked back to my car—or try to because the sidewalks are covered with a slick layer of snow and ice that even my boots have a difficult time navigating. Finally behind the steering wheel a minute later, I start my car back up, strip off my hat, toss it onto the dash, then take off Pebbles's sweater, which is soaked with snow, and put him in his bed before placing his blanket over him.

I unzip my coat and tuck it behind me, then hold my hands in front of the heater vent and pray for my fingertips to warm up. Even though it gets cold in Oregon, I swear the cold here feels different, and I'm not used to it.

After I've warmed up, I grab my cell phone and send a quick text to Cybil letting her know that I wasn't kidnapped and another to my parents letting them know what is going on before Cybil can beat me to it. A minute later my cell phone beeps with a message from Cybil with a simple heart, and a second later a text comes through from my dad just saying that he loves me and to make sure to keep him and Mom in the loop.

When I've finished texting my dad back, I let out a deep breath, then look at the building out in front of me and wonder for the millionth time if I'm making the right decision in moving to Montana and leaving my parents back in Oregon. Part of me knows that it's what is best for me, a fresh start, a do-over even, but it doesn't feel right. I've lived my entire life with my parents no more than a five-minute drive down the road, and now they are going to be hours away. Not to mention I don't exactly have a job and will be living with Cybil and Tanner until I find a place for myself, something that I'm not sure I'm looking forward to.

Don't get me wrong—I'm happy to be able to spend lots of time with Cybil, who I've missed like crazy and actually miss living with. Some of my best memories are from when we were young and she and I shared a bedroom after her mom passed away from cancer and she moved in with us.

And I'm really looking forward to being closer to my niece, who is adorable and the most perfect little girl, and I'm even happy to hang with Tanner, who is a really good guy.

But I'm not looking forward to living under the same roof as my best friend and her husband, who are grossly in love, and even though their house has lots of space, there is not going to be a way to escape them and their perfect coupledom. It's not that I'm not really happy for Cybil—I'm glad that she found someone perfect for her. It's just seeing her so happy and in love is an unwanted reminder of what I don't have and probably never will.

Not with my luck anyway.

Shaking my head at my own depressing thoughts, I pull up one of my favorite murder-mystery podcasts and press play on the latest episode, before I pull my coat from behind me and lean my chair back, using my jacket as a blanket. As the story plays, I watch the snow cover the windshield and pray that Maverick is okay and that he's not too far away.

Chapter 2

JADE

I blink my eyes open when I feel Pebbles crawl onto my chest, digging his tiny paws into my skin while he whines. "It's okay, baby." Holding him against me as the wind outside howls, I sit up to look around, not seeing anything through my windows, which are all now covered with what appears to be a thick layer of snow. Not sure how long I was sleeping, I grab my phone to check the time, and my eyes widen when I see that it's almost one in the morning.

Four hours. It's been four hours since I talked to Cybil, four hours since Maverick was supposed to be on his way to me. After pulling up Cybil's number, I press call and curse when my phone beeps in response. Glancing at the bars, I see then that I have no service. None. How that's possible when I had it earlier is anyone's guess, but I don't now.

Dropping my cell into the cup holder, I move Pebbles back to his bed and put on my coat along with my hat. There were more than a few cars in the lot when I got here, so if my car is now covered with snow, there will be no way for Maverick to spot it among all the other ones. Not that I know for sure that he knows what kind of car I'm in, but knowing my best friend, he does.

I push open the door—or try to, but it's like pushing up against sludge. The one good thing that happens is that the snow falls off the driver's window, allowing me to see outside, not that I see much—the bright lights that were lighting the parking lot for the rest area are now dark. All I can see is snow and more snow still falling steadily from the sky, and even though I have no desire whatsoever to get out of my car, I shove on my door until I'm able to open it enough to get out.

Pulling my hat down as far as it will go on my head, I shut the door, then wrap my arms around myself and walk back to my trunk through the snow, which is halfway up my calves. I might not know much about cars, but I do know that a blocked tailpipe is never a good thing under any circumstances.

Finding that the snow around it is mostly melted away, I kick it away farther, then look around. There are a few semitrucks still idling with their lights on, and judging by the unmarked snow covering the road, no one has been through here, so it's my guess that Maverick hasn't passed by and missed me, something that doesn't make me feel better at all, because now I'm worried about him.

I let out a deep breath and watch it curl up in front of me like a reminder of how cold it is, then get busy clearing the rest of my windows with the sleeve of my jacket, since the snow-remover brush I do have is under all the boxes and things in my trunk. Once I've got my windows mostly cleaned off, I hustle back around to the driver's side, colder now than I was before and also wet, which is not a good combination.

After I'm back behind the wheel and have my jacket and hat off, I glance down at the dash and feel my heart drop into the pit of my stomach. My gas tank was about half-full when I pulled off the highway, but it's now teetering on *E*, meaning I will soon be out of gas, without a phone and trapped in a blizzard with no way to escape and nowhere to go.

When Pebbles whines from my side, I reach over and cover his head with my hand, trying to come up with some kind of plan. I don't know how long my car will continue to idle, and I really can't risk shutting it off, because if I do, I don't know if it will start back up again. I look over my shoulder into the back seat at my suitcases there and lick my lips before I twist around in my seat and start dragging out clothes. When the gas eventually does run out, if I have on a few more layers, I should be able to keep myself warm. Then when morning comes, I can make my way to one of the trucks and hope they have a phone or some way for me to get ahold of someone to come and help me.

I'm sure at this point Cybil is probably freaking out, and knowing her, she's talked to my parents, so they are as well. Shoving my seat all the way back, I take off my boots and struggle out of my wet jeans and socks, something that is only made that much more complicated with the lack of space. Breathing heavy, I start to put on a pair of black leggings, then scream at the top of my lungs when I look over, finding a dark, shadowy figure standing outside my window.

"Jade." A deep voice cuts through the sound of my own pounding heart, and I focus on his face—not that I can see much of it with his black beanie pulled down over his ears and the collar of his jacket covering his lower jaw. *Maverick* . . . of course he would find me with my pants down around my ankles.

"I'm changing," I shout as he steps closer to the window, allowing me to see him more clearly, and I struggle to get my tight leggings up my thighs as fast as humanly possible, which isn't fast at all in the confined space.

"Sorry it took me so long."

"Ugh, it's okay." I lift my hips off the seat to get my pants up over my ass, then turn to the window and press the button to roll it down a bit. "Hey," I pant, and even though I can't see him well at all, I still catch the white of his smile.

"Hey." His voice is soft. "Are you ready to get out of here?"

"Yeah, I need to put on my shoes and stuff." I lean back to make room for Pebbles, who has walked across to my lap in order to get closer to Maverick.

"What do you want me to take to my truck?" he asks as Pebbles stretches up and rests his legs on the ledge of the window. "You might be stuck with me a couple days." He reaches in to pet the top of Pebbles's head.

"What?" My heart starts to pound for a completely different reason. Because again, I *know* him but do not really *know* him, and as I mentioned, he's seriously attractive.

"Roads are shit, and when this storm passes, it's supposed to freeze."

"So I won't be able to make it to Cybil's?"

"Not tonight, not sure about tomorrow either."

"Oh." I glance back at my suitcase, which is now open, with clothes exploding out of it. "I need to repack my bag; I had to change and was planning on putting on a few more layers since my car is just about out of gas," I tell him, and he smiles again, this time up close. Darn, but he has a great smile.

"All right, while you repack, I'm gonna grab a gas can from my trunk and fill up your tank so the gas line doesn't freeze while your car is parked here the next day or so."

"Okay, sure," I agree, figuring he knows what he's talking about.

"Close the window," he orders, removing his fingers from the top of Pebbles's head and stepping back. I do as instructed, not that it's something I need to be told to do—the cold air is enough of a reminder.

I watch him in my side mirror as he walks back to a seriously huge pickup truck that is idling behind me before I pick up Pebbles and place him back on his bed. Not surprisingly, it takes a few minutes to get my stuff packed and my suitcase zipped since I don't have the option of sitting on it to get it closed this time around. By the time that I'm finished and have gotten my socks, boots, and jacket on, he's put in enough gas to raise the dial above *E* in my car and pulled his truck into the spot next to me.

"Thanks for doing this," I tell him when I open my door and get out with my cell phone and Pebbles in my arms.

"It's not a big deal."

"I'm pretty sure that driving in the middle of a blizzard to rescue a chick you don't really know is the definition of a big deal." I listen to him chuckle as he opens the door to his truck and holds it for me to get in. Not that I do that; instead I place Pebbles on the seat, then turn back to my car so that I can help him with my stuff—or that's my plan anyway. What actually happens is I run face-first into his very firm chest, then grab onto him to keep from falling on my ass when my feet slip on the snow under me.

"I got you." His arms wrap around me as the scent of pine and musk fills my senses. Tipping my head way back, I look up at him, realizing then just how tall he is. I also can't help but think he's even better looking from this angle. His jaw even more chiseled, his lips even more full, and his cheekbones that much more pronounced. I would not normally use the word *pretty* when describing a man, but he is pretty in a very masculine way.

"Thanks."

"No problem." His hands move to my shoulders, then down my arms. "How about you let me worry about getting your crap from your car, and you just stay with your dog."

"It's not crap," I tell him, and he takes a step toward me, leaving me no choice but to take a step back or be pressed even tighter against him.

"All right, your stuff." He takes another step toward me, and I take another back.

"I can help."

"Or you can stay put." He shakes his head, and the next thing I know, his hands are moving from my arms to my waist, my feet are off the ground, and my ass is on the seat.

"You . . . you just picked me up," I sputter, now eye to eye with him or just about anyway, which shows just how tall he really is.

"Do you just want your suitcase, or is there anything else you need?" he asks, and I look around the interior of his truck, which is really fricking nice and smells like him.

"You picked me up." I turn back to him, still stunned that he was able to lift me off the ground with ease. I wouldn't say that I'm a large woman, but I'm definitely not tiny.

"Pippi, what do you want from your car?"

"Pippi?"

"Longstocking." He tugs on one of my red braids, and I blink at him. "It's an old TV show."

"Oh."

"So what do you want from your car?"

"My suitcase, purse, and the bag behind my seat with all of Pebbles's stuff in it."

"Got it. Tuck in your feet." He takes a step back, and I swing my legs into the truck before he slams the door shut and walks back to my car. Instead of watching him do what he's doing, I search for my pup, finding him curled up in the driver's seat, sound asleep. Leaving him for now, I take off my still-wet coat and hat and turn up the heat.

"Anything else you want before we take off?" Maverick asks after opening the back door of the truck and placing my bags on the back seat.

"Not that I can think of." I turn to look over my shoulder at him, then worry my bottom lip. "Do you think that my stuff is going to be okay until I can come pick up my car?"

"Do you have anything of value in there?"

"My whole life is in my car, or the most important stuff is anyways," I admit, and without a word, he shuts the door, goes back to my car, and opens the driver's door before leaning in to pop the trunk. I start to roll down the window to tell him that he doesn't need to do what I know he's about to, but the truth is I would be devastated if anything happened to my things. Everything that is in my car has sentimental value, since I left all my furniture and house stuff in my parents' garage, where it will be until I find a job and a place of my own. As he puts the few boxes from my trunk in the back seat with my bag, I check to see if I have phone service, finding that I still don't.

"All set?" he asks after opening the driver's door a minute later, and I reach over for Pebbles, who is not happy about being moved.

"Yes, and thank you again."

"It's not a big deal." He takes off his hat, which is covered with snow, and tosses it into the back of the cab; then his jacket follows suit, leaving him in a tight thermal with buttons at his neck.

"Again, it is a big deal." I hold on to Pebbles a little tighter when he tries to get away from me to get to Maverick. "I don't have any cell service; do you?" I ask him as he backs out of his parking space.

"I didn't when I hit the mountain." He passes me over his phone from the cup holder, and I stare at it. "You can check; the code's one two three four."

Using his pass code, I unlock his cell and see that he has one bar. "Do you have Cybil's number?"

"No, but if you call Tanner, he'll be there with her," he tells me, so I go to the contacts and press call on Tanner's number, only to have the phone beep in my ear.

"There must be a tower down or something." I place his phone back in the cup holder between us. "I hope Cybil isn't freaking out."

"You can call her when we get to my place," he says, and I press my hand against my stomach, which flutters with nervousness at the mention of his place.

"How far do you live from here?" I ask as he pulls out onto the highway, which is completely empty except for his truck.

"On a clear day thirty minutes. Not sure how long it will take to get back to my place now, but it shouldn't take the three hours it took me to get to you."

"Three hours."

"The only turnaround after the rest stop was an exit about twenty miles back, and since I was on the opposite side of the highway with no clear way to turn around after I passed you, I had to wait to take it."

"I feel like I need to thank you again."

"You don't," he assures me quietly before turning up the radio. Figuring that's his way of telling me that he's done talking, I turn my attention to the road ahead of us, ignoring or at least trying to ignore the anxiousness in the pit of my stomach.

Chapter 3

MAVERICK

After parking in front of my house, I shut down the engine, then turn to study Jade, who passed out about an hour ago. Before tonight I never noticed how pretty she is. Then again, I've only spent a handful of hours with her, and we've never been alone or even had time to talk. Reaching across the space between us, I grasp her biceps and give it a squeeze, watching her lashes flutter open before she turns her head my way.

"We're here."

"I fell asleep," she says, sleepily sitting up. "What time is it?"

"After three." I unhook my belt, then reach into the back seat to grab my coat and hers.

"You must be exhausted."

"I'm good." I put on my jacket and wait for her to finish getting hers on before I open the door to get out. Then I stop by my open door to meet her gaze. "Do you need anything besides your suitcase and the bag with the dog food in it tonight?"

"No, that should be good." She yawns as I hop out and head around the hood to the passenger side. I open her door and shake my head when I find that she's putting a lime-green turtleneck sweater on her dog. "Hey, don't look at him like that. You're going to give him a complex."

"I'm not judging him. I'm judging you," I tell her, helping her down as she laughs.

"Well, don't, because he'd freeze if I didn't put something on him."

"What did dogs do before humans came along?"

"I think they were wolves, so my guess is they were accustomed to being outside in the elements. Pebbles is not a wolf, and he doesn't even have much fur to keep himself warm, so thank goodness I can help him out." She kicks away a small area in the thick snow and sets her pup down, ordering him to potty, which he does on command. "So this is your place?" She picks him up when he's finished and I've grabbed her bags from my back seat.

"This is it." I walk with her up to the front porch of my two-bedroom, two-bathroom log home. "It's not much right now, but over the next three years I plan on building another house farther back on the property and using this cabin for friends and family when they come to visit."

"How much land do you have?"

"A little over twelve acres." I let her in the front door, and she stops to take off her boots and coat while I do the same. "I wanted more land than this, but I didn't want a place so far out of town that getting milk on a Saturday morning would be a hassle."

"My parents are on seventy acres and about thirty minutes outside of town. It's always an adventure anytime they need anything from the store." She waits for me to hang up my coat before she follows me down the short hall into my kitchen.

"This is it." I motion to the kitchen and living room. "Like I said, there isn't much to it."

"It's nice." She looks around, then stops at the picture window in the living room, where you can see part of the forest beyond my house with the help of the floodlights I have hooked up. "I bet the view out this window is beautiful during the day."

"It's not as nice as the view where I plan on building. Maybe if it's not too cold tomorrow, I'll take you up there on the snowmobile," I say, then wonder why the fuck I said that. No one, not even Tanner or Blake, has been up to where I plan on placing my house.

"I'd like that." She smiles, then looks down at her feet, and I'm surprised to see Caz wrapping herself around her ankles. "You have a cat?"

"No."

"No." She gives me an adorably confused look as Caz jumps up onto the back of the couch to get closer to her.

"This place was hers before it was mine. She came with the house."

"Your cat came with the house?" She laughs, getting closer so that she can pet her.

"Careful."

"She's sweet." She glides her hand down the cat's back, and Caz's spine arches like she wants more.

"She must like you. The only time she ever comes to me is when she wants a treat."

"That's because she's a smart girl." She rubs behind Caz's ears. "She knows that if she gives you too much attention, you'll take it for granted and forget that you need to give her something in return."

"That sounds like you're speaking from experience," I say, and she shrugs before meeting my gaze.

"Do you mind if I let Pebbles roam?" she asks on a yawn, covering her mouth.

"Nope." I head for one of the doors off the living room. "I only have bunk beds in my guest room. I hope that's okay."

"I'd sleep on the floor if that's all you had." She walks across the room to meet me, and I place her bag inside the room where my nephews have slept when they've come to visit me.

"The bathroom is down the hall where we came in, and there's towels and stuff in there if you want to shower. I think there might even be a fresh toothbrush in the linen closet, but I'm not sure."

"I have one of those." She pats the top of her suitcase. "Thank you again. I'm seriously going to bake you a dozen cookies as soon as I have access to an oven."

"You can bake?"

"No." She laughs, making me chuckle. "But I'm the best store-bought-cookie-dough baker around."

"I'm looking forward to experiencing that then." I smile and shake my head when she yawns once more. "Get some sleep. I'll see you in the morning."

"I should call Cybil and let her know I'm here."

"The house phone is in the kitchen on the wall. Last I checked, there was still no cell service." I head for the door, then stop and turn to face her. "If you wake in the morning before me, make yourself at home; coffee is in the pantry, and there's eggs and shit in the fridge to eat. With any luck, the freeze won't happen, and I'll be able to get you up to Cybil and Tanner's place tomorrow."

"Sure." She bends to pick up her dog and then holds him against her chest. "I'll see you in the morning."

"See you tomorrow," I tell her before going out into the living room and shutting shit down, leaving just enough light for her to see where she's going so she doesn't run into the furniture or trip over her dog or Caz. Once I'm done, I head for my room, strip down to my boxers, and get into bed. I don't know how long I lie there awake, but I don't fall asleep until after I hear her make her phone call, shower, and shut her bedroom door.

∼

"Pebbles, stop it!" I hear shrieking as a dog yaps, and my eyes fly open. "Oh my God, you're going to get yourself killed, you idiot! That's a bear!"

"What the fuck?" I sit up and flip on the lamp next to my bed, then quickly get up and throw on a pair of sweats from the chair in the corner of the room. After grabbing my gun from the top drawer in my dresser, I head out of the room and run down the hall to the front of the house, where I can hear Jade yelling at the top of her lungs and her dog barking.

Shoving the front door open, I curse when I find Jade, in nothing but a long T-shirt with an oversize flannel over it, chasing her dog around the base of a tree and a black bear clinging to one of the upper branches like he might take out the dog and Jade with one swipe of his claws if given the chance.

Without thinking, I rush through the snow, sweep an arm around Jade's waist, lift her up off the ground, and carry her kicking and screaming for her dog to the porch. "Stay," I order her and catch her eyes widening right before I spin around and head back into the snow. "Pebbles," I clip, and her dog stops barking and drops to all fours to focus on me. "Come." Like he doesn't know which to choose, his gaze swings between the bear and me. "Now," I bark. That gets his attention, and with his head ducked he hops toward me through snow almost taller than he is. When he gets close enough to grab, I pick him up, head up to the front porch, and pass him off to Jade before urging her into the house and closing the door.

"He's never done that before," she whispers, holding her pup against her chest, her body shaking from either the cold or the adrenaline dump. Probably both.

"What were you thinking, running around outside half-dressed without shoes?" I ask as I place my gun up on the shelf above the coat rack before I turn to face her.

"I'm fine."

"You're not." My jaw twitches as I take in the sight of her smooth, creamy skin, which is red from the cold, and her feet, which look burnt from the freezing temperatures outside.

"I'm fine," she repeats, and I meet her gaze, feeling anger like I haven't felt before. Irrational maybe, but then again, maybe not; who knows what the fuck could have happened if I hadn't heard her yelling.

"There was a fucking bear out there, Jade. What the fuck was that?" I shout, pointing at her.

"I obviously didn't know there was a bear out there, Maverick, or I wouldn't have let my dog outside," she shouts back, then slaps my finger away. "Don't point at me."

"Use your brain."

"You did not just say that." She takes a step toward me, putting a finger against my bare chest. "I didn't ask you to come out there, and you don't need to be a jerk to me. Do you think I wanted to run outside when there was a fricking bear out there?" She shakes her head from side to side, causing her wild red curls to swing this way and that. "No, I fricking didn't, but I also didn't want that bear to eat my dog." Her voice cracks on the word *dog*, and tears fill her eyes. "Great, now I'm crying, you jerk."

Cursing under my breath, I yank her against my chest and circle my arms around her, ignoring the urge I have to wrap my hand in her long hair, tip her head back, and kiss her. "It's okay, it's done, you're safe, and so is Pebbles."

"There was a bear," she says to me or herself as she burrows her face into my chest. "Aren't they supposed to be hibernating?"

"It's too early in the year yet for them to hibernate. They don't bed down until November, December."

"Oh." She leans back and wipes the tears from her cheeks; then her eyes go from my abs down to my bare feet. "You came out without shoes."

"I didn't have time to get any on. You scared the shit out of me."

"Sorry about that." She takes a step back, her gaze shooting to my chest and abs before her eyes lock with mine once more, and she fiddles with the bottom edge of her shirt. "I think . . . I think I'm going to take a shower to see if I can warm up."

"Did you eat breakfast?"

"No." She shakes her head and glances around like she's suddenly nervous. "Not yet. I just got up."

"I'll make some coffee and find some food for us. Did you talk to Cybil last night?"

"I did; she said she was going to find a tow truck company to pick up my car and take it to her place, since it might not make it with the little bit of gas in it."

"All right, I'll check the weather and see if I can find out how the roads are."

"Cool . . . awesome." She licks her lips, her eyes dropping once more as she takes another step back. "I'm just going to get some clothes."

"Sure." I watch her rush away and bite my bottom lip to keep from laughing. Fuck, but she's cute when she's flustered, but there is no fucking way I'm going there. Not with her.

Chapter 4

JADE

Sitting at the counter in Maverick's kitchen while he makes us breakfast, I watch him, completely fascinated by the dimples above his ass and the way his biceps flex as he flips pancakes or when he lifts his coffee to take a sip. I've been trying to keep my eyes off him, but the whole him-being-shirtless thing is making that almost impossible to do. I mean, not that I have any issue with him not wearing a shirt; he's just a lot fully clothed, so when he's half-naked, I feel like my brain has short-circuited.

"Jade," he calls, and I pull my eyes off the tattoo that takes up his left shoulder and focus on his face, which is no better for me to look at, not with the way his dark hair has fallen over his forehead or the morning shadow covering his jaw making his lips look even fuller. "Did you hear me?"

"No?" My nose scrunches, and his lips tip up into a roguish grin.

"I asked if you were good with taking the snowmobile out after breakfast, since you're stuck here at least for a few more hours."

"Oh, sure, that sounds fun." I pick up my cup of coffee to take a sip. "And thank you for letting me stay and for agreeing to take me up to Cybil's when the roads clear."

"You don't have to keep thanking me." He places a few pancakes on a plate, carries it over to where I'm sitting, and passes it to me. "I have maple syrup or regular."

"Do you have honey?"

"I think so." He walks to one of the cabinets and opens it up, and after moving a few things around, he pulls down a full bottle of honey and brings it over to me.

"Thanks."

"No problem." He goes back to the stove and begins making his own plate.

"So are these kinds of storms normal here?" I ask him while slathering butter on top of my stack of fluffy pancakes.

"Maybe not normal for this time of year, but the winters here can be harsh. If you really are planning on sticking around, you might want to think about getting a different car."

"My car isn't horrible in the snow when I have the snow tires on it; I just haven't changed them out this year yet." I cut into the pancakes, and my mouth waters. "And I would have made it here yesterday just fine, but I stopped at a trading post and lost track of time."

"Got it." He comes over and stands across from me with his plate, dumping a ridiculous amount of syrup on top of his stack of pancakes.

"Besides, a new car isn't a priority right now; getting a job and place of my own is."

"I thought that you were going to help Cybil out with her purse thing." *Purse thing.* I have to smile at his very male description. The truth is Cybil is an artist. A few years ago she decided that she was going to make herself a vegan-leather handbag, and the first time she wore it out, people were asking where she got it, and not long after that she started selling them locally in Oregon and online. Now people all over wear her designs; even some well-known celebrities carry her bags.

"Cybil doesn't really need my help; she just feels bad for me, so she offered me a job to help me out. And even though I appreciate it, it's not what I want to do with the rest of my life." I shrug, trying to ignore the tightness in my throat. "I had my dream job; being my own boss and working around books all day is what I always wanted to do. I need to find a way to get that back."

"You'll get there," he says softly, and I lift my eyes to his.

"I hope so." I take a bite of pancake and just barely avoid moaning because it's so good. I figured when he said he was going to make pancakes that they were going to be from a box, so I was surprised to see him making them from scratch, and I'm even more surprised by how good they are.

"Good?" he asks when I take another bite, and all I can do is nod as I chew.

"They put even my mom's pancakes to shame," I tell him after I swallow, and he grins. "Not that I will ever admit to saying that, so I'll deny it if you ever bring it up."

"Your secret is safe with me," he assures me, picking up his cup. "How is your mom doing?"

"She's good," I say, knowing he's asking because my mom had a heart attack a while back, around the time that Cybil and Tanner got together. "Her doctor says that as long as she keeps doing what she's doing, she should be okay. I really think that Cybil insisting that she go to a mostly plant-based diet has really helped a lot."

"Cybil was worried about her," he says, and I nod in agreement, thinking that's an understatement. Cybil considers my parents hers, so when my mom ended up in the hospital, it didn't just affect me; it affected her as well. Maybe even more so, since she lost her mom when we were just teens, and the fear that came from even thinking of losing mine was a lot for her to handle. "I'm glad she's doing all right."

"Me too."

"Are your mom and dad still looking for land up here?"

"Always." I sigh.

"I bet even more now that you're going to be here."

"No." I laugh. "Don't get me wrong—they are happy that I'm going to be here when they do move, but right now all they really care about is being closer to their first grandbaby. Cybil and I no longer factor into any of their decisions."

"Claire is a cute kid, so that's understandable."

"She's the cutest," I agree. "Did you see her little teeth?"

"I did. Got about a dozen photos from Tanner the day they popped out."

"Aww, he's a proud daddy."

"He is," he agrees, and I tip my head to the side.

"What about you—are your parents close by?"

"Dad's in New Mexico. I'm not sure where my mom is; I haven't spoken to her in a few years."

"I'm sorry."

"That's life." He lifts one shoulder. "I have a sister in Seattle. She has twin boys; they come during the school holidays and hang out if I'm not working."

"I was wondering why you had bunk beds. I thought that maybe when you were feeling nostalgic about your military days, you would sleep in your guest room," I tell him, and his head falls back as he laughs.

"No, I don't miss those days." He motions to my plate. "Are you done?"

"Since it would be inappropriate to lick the plate, I guess so." I get another smile before he takes my plate and his to the sink.

"After I clean up, I'll get dressed, and we can head out." He looks at me over his shoulder. "You might want to put on a few more layers; it's cold out and even colder when you're heading through the snow with the cold wind hitting you."

"How long is the ride to where we are going?"

"Depending on the snow and if any trees fell overnight, maybe twenty minutes. Hopefully by the time we get back, it will have warmed up enough to get some of the ice off the roads so I can get you up to Tanner's place."

"Great." I hop down off the stool I'm on and head for the room I stayed in last night. I find Caz asleep on the upper bunk when I enter and walk over to rub the top of her head before I dig through my bag for a pair of my baggy sweats and another long-sleeved thermal and put both on. Once I'm dressed, I find Pebbles where he's fallen asleep on the couch and take him outside to potty, this time making sure to use his leash because I'm not an idiot. When I get back inside, Maverick is dressed in jeans with a navy-blue sweatshirt, and even though I tell myself that I'm not disappointed that I don't get to look at him in all his shirtless glory anymore, I know that's a lie.

"Ready?" he asks when he spots me in the living room taking off Pebbles's sweater.

"Yep." I follow him to the door and put on my hat and coat, then startle when he grabs one of my hands and lifts it between us. "What . . ."

"Your hands will freeze if you don't have gloves on," he says, cutting me off before I can ask what he is doing, and begins to put one large mitten on my hand, then uses the tie on the wrist to tighten it so it doesn't fall off before doing the same to the other. "All set."

He lets my hand go and opens the door. I walk past him with my palm pressed against my stomach, which is fluttering, and head down the steps. When we reach the yard, he walks around the side of the house, and I notice then that there is a large shed just out of sight. I stand back as he opens the door and watch him as he uncovers a large black snowmobile. Until this minute I never realized how big they were, but up close they are huge, just about the size of the Jet Skis my parents own.

Once he has it started, he drives it out of the shed, then hops off and heads back into the metal building. He appears a minute later with two shiny black helmets. I take one from him and put it on over my hat, since it's big enough, then fuss with the buckle under my chin until he swipes my hands away.

"I would have got it."

"Now it's done." He chucks me under my chin when he's finished, and I try to be offended that he just used that whole big-brother-little-sister move on me, but seriously, I'm sitting here thinking how hot he is, and he's chucking me under my chin like I'm a little kid. "Are you ready?"

"As ready as I will ever be." I watch as he gets on the machine, and then he motions for me to get on behind him, something I thankfully do with ease. "Now what?" I wrap my hands around his sides. Or I try to, but it's awkward with the mittens, which are about three sizes too big.

"You're going to have to hold me a little tighter than that." He takes hold of my hands and pulls them forward to rest on his stomach, a move that causes my legs to spread wider and the space between us to become nonexistent. "Now if you need me to stop, just tap me, since I won't be able to hear you over the engine."

"Okay," I agree right before he revs the engine and puts the motor in drive. As we take off, I tuck the side of my face against his back and take in the scenery. It looks like a fairy tale with the freshly fallen snow covering the green branches of the trees and the white covering the ground as far as the eye can see.

If I were with anyone else, someone who's shown even an iota of interest in me, I would think this whole thing was really romantic, but that's not what this is. Even without words he's made that clear.

It's probably better that way. I have always been reckless in my pursuit of happiness and men, and I would never want to make things awkward for Cybil or Tanner. And since I have absolutely zero luck when it comes to dating, I know it wouldn't be long before it blew up in my face anyway.

When he starts to slow down a while later, I drag my cheek off his back to look around. He was not wrong when he said that the view up here was better than the one out the living room window of his house. From here you can see the mountains off in the distance and the valley below, with homes scattered few and far between, only really visible now because of the smoke escaping from their chimneys.

"This is it." He turns to help me off after I let him go, and I sink into the snow as I hop off, then lift my chin when he nudges it up so that he can get off my helmet.

"This is just . . . wow." I glance over at him as we walk toward one of the trees closer to the view. "Please tell me that this is going to be the view from your bathtub."

"I don't plan on putting in a bathtub," he says, coming to stand next to me, and my nose scrunches in disappointment because there is nothing better than taking a bath. Even Tanner, who is a total badass, takes baths with Cybil, and he reads to her while they are soaking. "This is where the deck is going to be."

"Are you going to put a hot tub on the deck?" I ask, looking up at him, and he shakes his head no.

"Well, you should." I cross my arms over my chest in an attempt to keep myself warm. It's cold, really fricking cold, and I know without a doubt that if I didn't have on the mittens he gave me, my hands would be frostbitten by the time we got back to his house. "You need someplace to hang out with your girl, and where better to hang out than the hot tub overlooking this gorgeous view, since you won't have a bathtub?"

"We can hang on the couch in the living room."

"Seriously?" I roll my eyes at him. "You want to hang out on the couch?"

"Would it be better if I said I would have a fire going in the fireplace?"

"Barely." I catch his smile and smile back. "So tell me about the layout—where is the kitchen going to be?"

"The kitchen will be here." He points at a spot near where he said the deck would be. "It's going to be open into the living room so that if I have family or friends over, everyone can hang out. There will be two bedrooms upstairs, including the master, but that will be the only one with a deck of its own, and another bedroom will be downstairs for guests or when I get too old to take the stairs."

"So you want to live here forever?"

"This was my dream," he tells me softly, turning to meet my gaze. "I didn't have much growing up, and me and my sister were moved around a lot as kids. I always wanted a place that was mine, with a little bit of land and a house big enough for the people I care about to be comfortable in."

"That's a good dream." I clear my throat to get rid of the itch of pain there, and he lifts his chin ever so slightly.

"It will be good when it's done." He walks off toward the snowmobile. "But there is a lot of red tape to go through, so it's taking longer than I thought it would."

"Some of the best things in life take time," I tell him as we stop, and he helps me put my helmet back on.

"You're right." He meets my gaze for a long moment, and my stomach flutters in response to the look in his eyes. A look I know I'm imagining, because it feels warm and good, like the kind of look you'd get right before a kiss. Taking a step back from him, I turn to get on the snowmobile. "But just so you know, I still think it would be better if you at least had a hot tub."

"Right." He laughs, putting his helmet on before he gets on the machine in front of me and pulls my arms around his waist. As we drive away from the place his house will one day sit, I let out a long breath and close my eyes and think that even without a hot tub or a tub, his place is going to be spectacular.

Chapter 5

JADE

With Maverick driving and Pebbles asleep on my lap, I watch out the window as we head up to Cybil and Tanner's house, which is just outside town. Thankfully the freeze that was supposed to happen didn't, and the sun came out just enough to melt some of the snow and ice off the roads, making it safe enough to drive. As we get closer, I can admit that I'm a little bummed that I won't be able to spend more time with the guy at my side, because even if he doesn't say much, he is good company. When we pull onto the familiar road that leads to Tanner and Cybil's house, giddiness fills the pit of my stomach, the same emotion I get every single time I'm about to see my best friend.

"Are you more excited to see Cybil or Claire?" Maverick asks, dropping his gaze to my bouncing leg for a moment before focusing on the road once more.

"Both of them." I laugh, and he smiles as the house comes into view.

"Just wait until I put the truck in park before you jump out. I don't need you getting run over."

"I would never jump out of a moving vehicle, but if I did, I know that you have to tuck and roll." I smile when he laughs and start to unhook my belt when I see Cybil step out onto the porch with my adorable niece in her arms and Tanner at her side.

"Hand me your dog." He reaches over, and I quickly pass him Pebbles.

"I think I might cry."

"Please don't," he mutters, putting his truck in park right before I push the door open and jump down out of the cab. As I head toward the steps, Cybil passes Claire off to Tanner, then rushes down the stairs to meet me. We crash into each other like we haven't seen each other in years, when in all honesty it's only been a couple of months.

"You're here." I hear the tears in her voice as she rocks me back and forth.

"I missed you so much." I hug her tight, then lean back to look at her. "You're still glowing."

"It's probably just the vomit I cleaned off my face with a diaper wipe earlier." She laughs, and I laugh along with her, then look at Tanner, who is watching us with a soft smile on his face.

"Hey." I walk over and greet him with a quick hug, then reach out to touch Claire's soft cheek. "Do you remember me?"

"Of course she remembers you; we FaceTime every day," Cybil assures me while taking Pebbles from Maverick.

"Ta ma ka da baba," Claire babbles as she lunges for me. I take her slight weight into my arms with ease and hold her against my chest, rocking her back and forth as I hug and kiss her chubby cheeks.

"She's gotten so big." I meet Cybil's gaze over the top of Claire's hat-covered head. "Didn't you tell her that she needs to stop growing?"

"We've had that conversation a few dozen times, but she never listens to us." She smiles, then leans into Tanner when he wraps his arm around her shoulders. I pull my attention off them when Claire starts to babble some more and reach over my shoulder. Turning around, I find Maverick a few feet away with his hands tucked into the front pockets of his jacket.

"You don't like him," I tell her, and she pounds her fist into my shoulder while kicking her legs.

"Mav is her favorite person," Cybil says to my back, and I look down at Claire and kiss her cheek before I walk her over to the man she is trying her hardest to get to. Once we are close, Maverick holds out his hands, and as soon as I hand her over to him, she curls into him, resting her head on his shoulder. I tell myself that my ovaries are not exploding as I watch him kiss the top of her head and hold her with a gentleness that comes from experience, but I know I'm lying. He looks good holding a baby, even better than he looks shirtless, and that's saying something.

"I should get my stuff." I turn to Cybil, and Tanner shakes his head.

"Let's leave it in the truck; we'll drive it down to the shop and unload it there."

"The shop." I plant my hands on my hips. "Are you already kicking me out of the house?" It's a joke. Kind of, because I know that the shop is actually Cybil's studio, a place Tanner set up for her so that she would have a quiet place to make her bags.

"Of course not." Cybil steps in front of her husband. "You can stay in the house with us if you want, but we just thought that you would be happier having your own space. Tanner and the guys finished renovating the shop a week ago, so I thought that since there is a bathroom and a kitchen there now, you could stay there. I mean, it's kind of like its own place, so you wouldn't have to stress about finding a place to rent until you're ready."

"What about when you're working? I know you like your own space."

"The living space is completely cut off from my shop; you have a door and everything. Plus, with you there, Claire won't be waking you up all hours of the night like she does us."

"I don't mind her waking me up."

"I know you don't, but I want you to be happy here so you'll stay," she says softly, and I shake my head at her before going to give her another hug. I know even with her having Tanner and Claire here, along with the group of friends she's made, it's been hard having my parents and me so far away from her.

"You're stuck with me," I tell her, kissing the side of her head before letting her go.

"Sorry all the hormones have made me a mess." She wipes the tears from under her eyes.

"Don't apologize. I cried this morning too."

"Why?" She takes my arm in hers and starts leading me up the stairs to the front door.

"Because Maverick yelled at me."

"He what?" She starts to spin around to look at him, and I laugh, tugging her with me into the house.

"He got upset that I was outside barefoot with a bear," I tell her, hearing Maverick chuckle.

"What?" she asks, sounding horrified.

"When I got up this morning, I let Pebbles out to potty, and next thing I know, there's a black bear coming around the corner of the house, and Pebbles, who thinks he's much bigger than he is, ran up to it barking and chased it up a tree. Then like an idiot, I ran out into the snow after him because he wouldn't listen to me and come back into the house. That's how Maverick found me, outside running around half-dressed trying to catch my dog."

"Oh my God." She laughs as I take a seat on one of the stools in the kitchen. "Thank goodness you and Pebbles are both okay."

"I know."

"Well, maybe we should think about putting a fence up near the shop. That way you can let him out without that happening again."

"I'll just use his leash; he's pretty good about not taking a year when I take him out, so I think it will be okay," I tell her, then look up at

Maverick when he comes to stand next to me, still holding Claire. "You want to come see Auntie Jade?" I hold out my hand, and she shakes her head no while she clings to him. "Don't you have to leave already?" I meet his gaze, and he grins at me like I'm being funny.

"I don't, but you can have her while Tanner and I take your stuff to your spot," he tells me, then looks at Tanner. "When is Jade's car going to be here?"

"Anytime. The guy who picked it up said that he'd be here before three," he answers, and Maverick lifts his chin, then hands Claire to me. Since she is not even a little interested in me holding her and is fighting me to get back to him, I kiss her cheeks to distract her and tickle her until she laughs. Tanner, taking that as his cue, heads for Cybil and gives her a quick kiss before he and Maverick both head out of the house.

"How did things go with you and Maverick?" Cybil asks as soon as we hear the door close, and I drag my attention off Claire to look at her.

"Fine. He's not the most talkative man I've ever met in my life, but he made me breakfast and took me up to where he plans on building his house, so that was nice."

"He's a nice guy; all the guys are. I think you're going to love it here once you're settled."

"I already love it here because you and Claire are here, so please don't stress about me being happy. I'm going to be fine," I assure her, and she studies me closely.

"I know you will." Her face softens as she looks at her daughter. "And who knows—maybe you'll find what I did here."

That's doubtful, but of course I don't say so. I mean, she won the life lottery on a fluke. Who else could have their fiancé break up with them weeks before their wedding, go on the couples retreat that she was supposed to go on with her ex, meet a guy like Tanner, fall in love, end up pregnant by accident, and then get married to the right guy? That's the kind of thing that only happens in the books I read; it definitely doesn't happen in real life, and it sure as heck would never happen to me. With my luck I would have ended up marrying the wrong guy and spent the rest of my life wondering why the heck I hadn't run when I should have. "My priority right now is to find a job and a way to open another bookstore. If I can do both those things, I will be happy."

"Well, I just might have some good news for you." She comes around to take Claire when the little girl reaches for her. "Do you remember Blake, Tanner's other partner?"

"Yeah, Tanner's other best friend, right?" I ask, thinking of the blond guy I met the last time I was in town. He and his fiancée both were so sweet and cute together.

"Yep, well, his fiancée's dad has decided that he's going to move his law practice to his house since he's not working as much as he used to, and his office is right on Main Street. I thought that maybe if you were interested, we could go check it out. It's not a huge space, but it would make a cute bookstore, and it's in the perfect location with lots of foot traffic."

"I don't really have the money to open another shop right now."

"You might not, but I do."

"I'm not letting you pay for me to open another shop." I shake my head in denial.

"I would also be doing it for myself. I figured that I could have a display there with a few of my bags, and I know there's a few other girls in town who make stuff and sell it online. I thought that it would be cool to have not only books but some stuff from local sellers."

"That would be cool," I agree, trying not to get my hopes up. "How would it work with us selling other people's stuff, though?"

"They'd give us a percentage of what they make off each item they have in the store. And if you think about it, they would have a vested interest in keeping people coming back, so I think it would be beneficial for all of us."

"I like that idea."

"Me too." She smiles, then asks, "I'm sure that the guys are done unloading all your stuff; do you want to go check out your new home?"

"Yes." I scoot off my stool, then find Pebbles where he's curled up next to one of the heater vents. Once I have him and have put his leash on him, Cybil, Claire, and I head out the back door and then walk the short distance to the shop, which is a huge metal building with a large rolling door and a smaller door on the side.

The building used to be where Tanner kept some of the equipment for the lodge that he's part owner of, but when Cybil agreed to move in with him, he renovated half of it for her. That way she would have a place to make her one-of-a-kind vegan-leather bags, purses that people from all over the world order because they truly are like pieces of art.

When Cybil lets us inside the building, we head through her workshop, where she keeps her sewing machine and all her materials, and go to the left, where there is another door. Since her hands are full with Claire, I open it for her and hear Tanner and Maverick talking. They stop as soon as we step inside.

"Were you guys talking about us?" she asks her husband, going over to him to pass off Claire, who's excited to see her dad after just a few short minutes.

"No, we were talking about the message that Mav and I just got from Blake."

"Is everything okay?" she asks.

"Yeah, but he's asking if we can all make it to the lake house at the end of next month. Him and Everly decided that they are going to have a small ceremony there but want to make a whole weekend of it, so we'd go on Friday; then Sunday would be the wedding."

"Oh." She looks at me, and I hold up my hand because I know she's thinking that since I'm here, she shouldn't go.

"Please do not even worry about me. I'll be just fine here on my own." I look around the space, which I didn't really get a chance to take in, then smile at Tanner. "You've got some skills. The last time I was here, all this was just rusty bare walls and a concrete floor."

"I had some help," Tanner tells me with a proud smile.

"Honestly, this place is nicer than the apartment I had in Oregon and maybe even bigger. The only difference is it's all one room." I motion to the bed just on the other side of where the couch and TV are set up in the middle of the room.

"That's why we put this in." He walks across the room to where the bed is and grabs ahold of what looks like a piece of metal folded against the wall and pulls. As he does, a wall on wheels unfolds, cutting off the bed from the rest of the room, making it feel like more of an apartment. "You can leave this open or keep it closed."

"That's so cool. Did you make it?" I ask because I can tell that it was custom built for the space.

"No, a friend of ours, Mason, did. He's a bartender in town but used to be a welder on the pipeline. You'll meet him at some point."

"Well, if your whole adventure-lodge business ever goes under, you guys could get into home remodeling and make a killing," I say, referring to their business, which is basically one of those places where they take people out into the woods and have them work on team-building exercises. It's not exactly my cup of tea, but Cybil did meet Tanner on one of their retreats for couples, a trip she was supposed to go on with her ex-fiancé but ended up taking alone, so it worked out for her.

"So what do you think?" Cybil asks.

"It's beautiful." I walk to the kitchen and open the fridge, which of course is already stocked with my favorite drinks and foods. I turn to look at my best friend, shaking my head. "You're going to spoil me, and I'm never going to leave."

"That's the plan." She comes over, wrapping her arm around my shoulder. "Do you want to see the best part of this place?"

"There's more?"

"Just one more thing." She pulls me along with her to a door on the opposite side of the bedroom area and opens it.

"Stop it." I rush to the bathtub that is placed at the end of a long, partially enclosed glass shower and get inside of it. "I have a bathtub."

"You do, but just so you know, I might use it sometimes." She gets in it with me so that we are sitting face-to-face. "Right now Claire knows exactly when I'm about to take a bath, so I never really get to enjoy mine and Tanner's."

"You can use this, or better yet I'll bring Claire down here so that you can enjoy your bath along with some alone time with your husband," I whisper, then smile when she blushes.

"I might just take you up on that offer," she says under her breath, eyeing Tanner when he and Maverick both walk into the room.

"Mav and I are going to head back to the house in case the guy bringing Jade's car shows up," Tanner says while helping Cybil climb out of the tub. "Do you want me to take Claire? That way you can help Jade get settled."

"I can unpack later." I get out after her. "We can all go back to the house."

"While we're there, we can figure out what to do for dinner. I was thinking that tacos sound good," Cybil says, then looks at Maverick. "Do you want to join us?"

"I would, but I got plans," he tells her, and I wonder if those plans involve a woman. I also wonder why I care. I shouldn't. I know I shouldn't, but that doesn't mean I don't.

"Next time." She hooks her arm with mine, and as we head back to the house, I ignore the way my stomach feels, because I should definitely not feel funny about him dating someone, especially when I've barely spent a handful of hours in his presence.

Chapter 6

JADE

I drive down Main Street in town with Cybil sitting in the passenger seat and search for a place to park. With Halloween just around the corner, everyone seems to have gone all out decorating for the holiday. It looks like a postcard with both sides of the street lined with brick buildings and antique-looking signs hanging above the doors, pumpkins painted on the windows, and ghosts suspended off the black lampposts that line the road.

"Oh, there's a spot." Cybil points to a car backing out a few feet ahead of us, so I flip on my blinker and wait for it to leave before I pull into the now-empty space.

"How far is the law office?"

"Just a minute's walk down the street." She motions to my left, so I grab my hat and put it on over my hair, then lift my purse from the back seat. After we get out, we meet on the sidewalk, then both walk quickly to get out of the cold.

"Can we stop and get a coffee when we're done?" I ask as we pass a coffee shop with a gold black bear etched into the glass window.

"Yes." She comes to a stop in front of a plain white door next to the coffee shop and turns the handle. "And if we do take this space, we'll have access to the best coffee in town every day, since it's right next door."

"This is it?" I look at the window next to the door and notice that it's got the blinds down and closed and no sign in the window.

"This is it." She opens the door, and when we step inside, the older woman sitting at the desk looks up and smiles at us.

"Cybil." She greets my friend with a warm, familiar smile. "Where is that baby of yours?"

"At home with her dad," Cybil says, then motions to me. "Sandy, this is my best friend, Jade; Jade, this is Sandy, Blake's grandmother."

"It's nice to meet you." I smile.

"You as well." She pushes out of her chair, then grabs her sweater, which is draped over the back, and puts it on. "Gene told me that you girls were coming to have a look around, so while you're here, I'm going to pop next door to grab a coffee."

"Sure," Cybil says, then asks, "are you still going to be working for Gene when he moves his office to his house?"

"Nope, I'm going to retire and spend some time with my new husband." She smiles. "We're thinking about buying one of those RVs and traveling around the US a few months out of the year."

"That sounds fun."

"I think so too." She winks and then gives Cybil's arm a squeeze. "Stop by next door when you're done and let me know."

"I will," Cybil tells her.

Then Sandy's eyes come to me. "It was nice meeting you, Jade."

"You too." I smile back, then watch her leave.

"So this is it." Cybil motions around the room, then heads through a doorway right behind the desk Sandy was at, and I find that it's another room not much bigger than the front one. "So what do we think?" Cybil asks as I go back into the front room and open a door there, finding a small bathroom.

"I like it, and it's bigger than the space I had back home. How do you feel about it?" The space is not overly large, but it does have potential.

"I like it too. I also wonder how difficult it would be for Tanner to take down the wall between the two rooms so that we can open up the space." She walks to the doorway between the rooms and looks from one side to the other. "If he can do it without too much trouble, it would really open up the space and give us a lot more options when it comes to the layout of everything."

"But can we do that?"

"What do you mean?" She frowns at me.

"I mean, we would be renting the space, and this building is old. I don't know that we can just take out a wall because we want to."

"Oh." Her frown grows deeper as she looks around once more. "Well, if we can't, we could put a couch back here along with some shelves for books, then another wall of shelves in the front, and use the rest of the space for the vendors who are going to be selling out of the store."

"How much is the rent on this place a month?" I walk to the window that looks out to the street and open the blinds.

"I think it's just about two thousand dollars, but that includes the electricity, water, and garbage."

"That's a lot of money, Cybil," I say quietly, turning to face her as my stomach sinks.

"Yeah, but it's also a great location right in the middle of town."

"I don't know." I shake my head.

"What don't you like about it?"

"It's not that I don't like anything about it. It's that I know how much it cost me to run my shop, and I also know how much money I was making. Even with the stuff I was selling out of the back room, I wasn't making a killing each month. Really, I was just getting by, and my rent was half the cost of this place."

"But that was there and this is here, and we won't just be selling books; we'll have lots of other stuff to sell."

"I get that, but I don't know that I'm comfortable jumping into this situation without having a solid plan. Right now we don't know what else we would sell here besides your bags and my books. We need to talk to the vendors you were telling me about and see what kind of stuff they would want us to have in the store so that we can get an idea of what kind of money they will be bringing in each month. If after we talk to them, we think that we can cover the rent each month with a little bit of a profit, we can move forward, but until then I think we need to wait." I let out a deep breath, then say quietly, "As much as I want this, I do not want to have it and then lose it because we can't afford the space and the overhead. Plus I still have to be able to survive, and eventually I'm going to need to find a place of my own, so I need to think about the cost of that as well."

My hands ball into fists at my sides as anxiousness makes my stomach churn. I've had such horrible luck these last few months, and I don't know what I would do if this failed and ended up costing my friend and others money. When I opened my bookstore, I was so sure that it would be a success that I didn't think about all the what-ifs. Now with that experience under my belt I understand how quickly you can go from profitable to in the red. I could easily blame the woman who found out about the back room in my shop and turned others against me, but there were lots of factors that went into me not being able to keep the shop open any longer, including me giving my nest egg to my ex only to have him refuse to give it back when I needed it to cover my rent for the shop. Not that I even know that I would have been able to keep the doors open much longer even with that money, since toward the end I was barely skating by each month.

"I told you that you could stay with us for as long as you want," Cybil says, dragging me from my thoughts, and I focus on her.

"I know you did, and I appreciate that, but I don't want to be Claire's weird aunt that lives in the shed behind her parents' house forever."

"It's not a shed."

"I know; I'm just joking. Kind of." I shrug. "The truth is if I continue to live my life like I have been the last five years, just hoping everything works out with no real plans for the future, there is a real possibility that I could end up the crazy aunt in the shed, and I really, really don't want that. I want to be able to afford a nice place to live and a vacation at least once a year, so it's time for me to grow up and to stop living for today when tomorrow is a possibility," I finish as she stares at me like I've grown another head. "So are you okay with us talking to the vendors you know and going from there?"

"Of course."

"Awesome." My muscles relax. "After that, if this place is still available, we'll figure out how to move forward."

"You know I love you, right?" She stops me as I head for the door, and I turn back around to face her. "I've always been envious of the fact that you've never been afraid to take chances, to jump without looking."

"Cybil."

"Don't stop doing that just because one thing didn't work out the way you thought it would."

"I'm not. I'm just being cautious and making sure that there is nothing that might impale me when I do jump," I tell her, and she nods before walking toward me.

"Since Tanner has Claire, what do you say we go have lunch? There's a great bar with awesome food just down the street from here."

"Perfect, and while we're there, I'll see if they're hiring." I open the door for us to leave.

"You are not going to work in a bar." She stops in front of me and rolls her eyes.

"Why not?"

"Because you have a problem with listening to people and you have a smart mouth. You'd last a week at most before you quit or got fired."

"Whatever," I mutter since she's not wrong. Still, when we leave the store, I put in an application at the coffee shop right next door, and then when we get to the restaurant, I ask for an application and fill it out on the spot. Neither place would be my ideal job, but money is money when you are broke.

~

Sitting on the couch at my place, I flip through the channels, trying to find something to keep me occupied until I go to bed, which might be sooner than later with how tired I am already. It's been a crazy few days between talking to potential vendors for the bookstore, looking for a job, and spending some much-needed auntie time with my niece. I feel like I've been going nonstop.

After settling on a documentary about an ancient group of people who lived in the Amazon rain forest, I shove my hand into the bag of popcorn I made, then shake my head when my cell phone beeps. Figures. After wiping off my buttery fingers on a piece of paper towel, I grab it and check the screen, seeing a number I don't recognize along with a message asking if I'm doing okay.

Me: Who is this?

I watch three little dots appear a moment later.

Unknown Number: Maverick

When I see his name, my stomach flutters, and I sit up a little taller while I stare at my phone, not sure how to respond. It's been three days since I last saw him, and I honestly didn't think I would talk to him again until Tanner and Cybil had one of the get-togethers that their friends are known for.

Me: How did you get my number?

I go to my contacts and add him onto the list so that I have him in my phone.

Maverick: Tanner gave it to me. Are you settling in okay?

Me: Yeah, for the most part anyways.

Maverick: Why for the most part?

Me: Because I don't have a job and that is kind of important LOL

Maverick: Have you looked in town?

Me: Yes

Maverick: No one's gotten back to you?

Me: Not yet

Maverick: Tanner mentioned that you and Cybil went and looked at a space for a bookstore. How did that go?

Me: Why are guys always bigger gossips than women?

Maverick: How did it go?

Figures that he would ignore my question.

Me: It went fine

Maverick: You didn't like it?

Me: I didn't say that, the space is awesome; the rent is just a lot more than I'm comfortable with. We are talking to some local vendors now to see if we can offset some of the cost.

Maverick: Everything will work out. So what are you doing tonight?

Me: I'm on my couch in my pajamas watching TV and eating popcorn.

Maverick: It's Friday.

Me: It is

Maverick: How long will it take you to get dressed?

Me: I'm already dressed

Maverick: Right, I'm headed your way, we'll go out for a drink.

A pity drink with him? No thank you.

Me: No thanks like I said I'm in my PJs and watching TV, I'm going to go to bed soon.

Maverick: Be there in fifteen

Me: Do not come here because I'm not leaving my house

Maverick: Make sure you're dressed.

Me: I'm serious, Maverick, do not come here because I'm not getting dressed or going out with you.

I press send on that text, then stare at my phone and wait for him to reply. When he doesn't, I shake my head and try to get comfortable. He might be the kind of guy who is used to telling women what to do and them doing it, but there is no way that I'm moving my ass off this couch, and he can't make me.

As the time ticks away, I try to focus on the TV, but all I can think about is that he's on his way here and my hair is a mess and I have about five pimple patches on my face. And the more of those thoughts that I have, the more annoyed with myself I become.

"Fuck," I yell, pushing up off the couch before I stomp to the bathroom. I might not get dressed, but I'm too vain to let him see me with my hair a total disaster and my face a mess. With quickness gained from years of experience, I put my hair up in a messy but cute bun on the top of my head, then remove the patches and moisturize my face. When I'm done, I don't look great, but I do look better than I did. I head back to the couch and start to sit down but stop when I hear pounding on the door. Knowing it's him, I head out of my apartment and through Cybil's shop and open the door. I wonder how a guy could possibly get hotter in less than seventy-two hours.

"You're not dressed?" His eyes drop to my tank top and sleep pants.

"I told you that I'm not going out."

"You need to get out of the house."

"I don't." I cross my arms over my chest when the cold air from outside soaks through my thin shirt, making me realize that I do not have a bra on.

"Get dressed, Jade."

"No, Maverick." I turn on my heel and head back into my apartment, where it's much warmer. "You wasted your time coming over here."

"All right, then I'll hang here with you," he says, following me across the room to the couch, and I swear my stomach drops to my toes. "What are we watching?" he asks, then picks up Pebbles when he comes over to say hi.

"We are not watching anything; you're leaving and going out with your friends, and I'm hanging here by myself watching TV, then going to bed."

"Are you always so stubborn?"

"I don't know. Are you always so annoying?" I snap, and he laughs like I'm being funny when I'm not.

"Come on, I know how it is to be new to a place and not really have anyone. Hell, when I was in the military, if I didn't have Tanner and Blake with me, I don't know what I would have done."

"I have Cybil."

"You do." He takes a seat on the couch next to me. "But she's married and has a baby. Her life and yours are not the same right now."

"Thanks for pointing that out." I glare at him before I grab my bag of popcorn off the coffee table and place it in my lap.

"I'm just saying you don't have to sit at home alone on a Friday night; you can go out and meet new people." He leans back, resting his ankle on top of his knee.

"And I appreciate your offer to take me out, and maybe another time I will take you up on your offer, but I'm not up to going anywhere tonight." Also I really am not interested in going out with him and watching women fall all over themselves to get his attention, which I'm sure is what would happen.

"Fair enough." He reaches for the bag in my lap and takes it without even asking and grabs a handful.

"Sure, I'll share my popcorn with you," I sass, watching him grin before he focuses on the TV.

"So what the hell is this that we are watching?"

"It's a documentary." I take the popcorn back from him. "And if you are going to insist on being here, please don't talk during my show." I get comfortable as close to the arm of the couch as I can get, trying with all my might to ignore the fact that he's here and that I like it. That ridiculous feeling in the pit of my stomach is back with a vengeance, and I know he's the one who's caused it. Stupid, I'm so stupid. I shouldn't have a crush on someone who doesn't like me as anything more than a friend. And I really hate feeling like I'm back in high school, crushing on the guy who doesn't even know I exist.

"Are you actually enjoying this?" His question cuts off my internal monologue, and I focus on him.

"Yes."

"It's boring."

"It's interesting. I love history."

"Why don't we put on a movie?"

"Don't you have some other woman you could be bothering right now?"

"Nope." He shrugs, then reaches for the remote.

"Do not change the channel."

"I think there's a new superhero movie out on demand." He ignores me and points the remote at the TV, so like any mature person I lunge for it. Of course he's fast and sees me coming, so I end up pressed chest to chest with him while he raises the remote up over his head just out of my reach.

"Give it to me," I demand, crawling on top of him trying to get it, but his arms are abnormally long—either that or mine are just short. With a huff of frustration and a whole lot of awareness, I press my hand against his chest and push back so that I'm kneeling on the couch next to him. "You're a jerk," I point out, breathing heavily as I pull the hair tie out of my hair, which is now hanging off the side of my head.

When he doesn't respond, I focus on him and find that he's looking at me like he hasn't before. My stomach turns over on itself, and I lick my lips, liking it a little too much when his gaze drops to my mouth for the briefest of moments before shooting to mine.

My muscles lock, and I brace myself for what I'm sure is to come, but the moment is broken when his cell phone starts to ring in his pocket.

"Shit." He shakes his head and pulls it out to glance at the screen before he looks at me once more. "I'm gonna head out."

"Yeah, cool." I fall back on my bottom as he pushes up off the couch.

"You got my number if you need anything."

"I do," I agree with a nod, watching him walk to the door and open it before turning to look at me once more.

"See you around."

"Yep." I watch him leave, then drop my face into my hands. I don't know what the heck that was, but I do know that he felt it too. I'm also pretty sure that if his phone hadn't rung, we would be making out right this minute.

Chapter 7

JADE

All my life I've considered myself to be someone who fits in pretty easily, but as I stand behind the counter of the Bear, the coffee shop I applied to right next door to what I hope will one day be my bookstore, I couldn't feel more out of place if I tried. At first I thought that Liam, the owner, who is old enough to be my grandfather, was taking pity on me by hiring me for this job. Now I think he just hired me to babysit his great-grandkids, Tony and Katie, who work here after school each day.

"What do you think about this?" Tony asks, shoving his cell phone in front of my face, and I watch a video of him doing some strange dance while he makes a cup of coffee. "Isn't it dope?"

"Totally dope."

"We should do one together. You have that whole hot-older-lady thing going on." He goes back to looking at his phone, missing the scowl I'm shooting his way. "I'm sure you and I could get a few thousand likes." He looks up at me. "Can you dance?"

"No." I go to where the broom is and grab it so that I can sweep up some of the coffee grounds and beans that have fallen onto the floor over the last couple of hours.

"Tony can totally teach you," Katie says from where she's sitting on the counter with her legs swinging. "He's really a good dancer." I'm sure she thinks that; then again, I've gotten the impression over the last few hours that Katie is Tony's biggest fan and vice versa.

"You know, as much as I love that idea, I don't think that's a part of my life plan at the moment."

"Please tell me that you're not one of those old people who thinks social media is stupid." Katie hops down when the bell for the door dings. "You can make, like, millions of dollars a year if people like your content."

"First of all, I'm not old, and second, is that really true?"

"Uh, yeah," Tony tells me as Katie starts to take the order from the couple who just walked in. "Our cousin Micky makes bank every month doing nothing but making videos of himself playing video games. And we have another friend who just posts pictures of herself holding products, and she is raking in the dough."

"I obviously chose the wrong line of work," I mumble under my breath as I grab the dustpan and Tony starts up the espresso maker. Once I'm done dumping the contents of the pan into the trash and washing my hands, I go to stand next to Tony and listen carefully as he walks me through the steps for the drink he's making.

In two days I will be on my own from early afternoon until Tony and Katie get out of school, so I need to learn how to run the espresso machine, and unlike the register, it's not something I've done before. After watching him make two somewhat complicated drinks, I take them over to Katie, and she hands them to the man and woman, then waves them off as they leave the store. One thing can be said about both kids: they do know what they are doing and are pretty professional.

"So if you don't dance, what can you do?" Katie asks me, taking the tip money out of the jar so that she can count it out.

"What can I do?"

"Yeah, like, what are you good at, what are you into? Can you sing?"

"No."

"Tell jokes?"

"No."

"Transform yourself into a goddess with makeup?" She rolls her head around on her shoulders while planting her hands on her hips like she's annoyed with me.

"Again, no. I like to read." I shrug.

"You could review books," she suggests.

"What?"

"You know, if you wanted to make a social media account, you could do one where you review books."

"No one wants to watch that." I shake my head.

"Apparently they do," Tony says, handing me his phone. "Just tap the screen to press play." I do, and a pretty blonde appears, holding a familiar-looking book; then for about a minute she raves about it, talks about her favorite scene, and gushes over the author. "That video got over a million views. She is for sure making money off of it."

"You think so?" I study the girl and watch the video again. "I could do that."

"You should do that but do it better." Tony takes his phone back. "I could show you how to do the dance trends that are happening now so that you get more followers."

"I don't think so." I hold up my hand and shake my head.

"Come on, we could do one, and if you hate it, I won't mention it ever again."

"I don't . . ."

"Where is your phone?" He cuts me off, and I point to where it's charging near the register.

"Great." He grabs it, starts to bring it to me, but stops and reads whatever is on the screen. "Who's Maverick?"

"What?" I snatch it from him, finding that Maverick sent me a message two hours ago.

"Is that your boyfriend?" Katie asks.

"No." I unlock my phone so that I can read his text, which asks how my first day at my new job is going, and since I haven't spoken to him since our last strange encounter, I know that he must be talking to Tanner about me again.

"So who is he?" Katie asks, looking over my shoulder at the screen.

"No one." I exit out of the message and hand my phone to Tony. As he does whatever he's doing, I go out to the main room and wipe down the small table, where there is milk, cream, sugar, and other coffee supplies. As I clean up, I wonder if Maverick asked Tanner how I'm doing or if Tanner just brought up me getting a job in conversation. My guess is the latter, since Maverick doesn't seem like the kind of guy who would ask something like that, even if he were curious.

"All right, you need a screen name," Tony calls out, dragging me from my thoughts.

"I don't know. Make something up."

"What about Red Books, you know, since your hair is red and you like to read?"

"Oh, I like that." Katie nods her approval, and I have to admit that is a pretty cool name.

"All right, now I'll pick a photo for you, and then we'll make your first video," Tony says, and I start to shake my head no. "You need content, plus remember this is your first one; you want to see if it's something you like."

"Fine." I give in.

"Do you have a book with you?"

"On my phone." I shrug.

"That will work." He goes back to focusing on my phone; then a second later his gaze meets mine. "Done, now let's get to dancing."

"Right now?"

"Yes."

"We're working," I point out, and he rolls his eyes.

"Do you see a line I don't? No one is in here right now. This is our slow time; things will pick back up around five, and we will be done by then."

"All right." I give in and follow him to the front of the shop, where there is more room to move around.

"Just follow me." He starts to break down the dance he wants me to learn in small steps, but I'm a fumbling idiot with two left feet. If Cybil were to see me right now, she would be laughing her ass off.

"I don't think that dancing is her thing," Katie says unhelpfully from where she is sitting on the counter facing us.

"Maybe we need some music. Toss me my phone," he tells her. She sends it flying through the air, and he catches it with ease. After starting up a song I've only heard a couple of times on the radio, he begins dancing again. I'm so caught up in trying to follow along with him I don't hear the door to the shop ding as someone comes in, but I do feel warmth on the side of my face like someone is watching me. Turning to see what's got my senses up, I find Maverick watching me, with his arms crossed over his chest, and my heart falls into my stomach.

"What are you doing here?" I ask, straightening from the awkward bent position the dance required me to be in, and rub my sweaty hands down the front of my jeans.

"You didn't text me back, and I was in town, so I figured I'd come to check on you."

"As you can see, I'm fine." I push my hair out of my face as Tony shuts off the song that was playing. "Did Tanner tell you I got a job here?"

"No, Cybil did when I went to the house to drop some stuff off."

"Oh." I tuck my hands into the back pockets of my jeans, feeling awkward.

"You haven't messaged since I saw you," he says quietly.

"Sorry, but in all fairness today is the first time you've messaged me."

"You're right," he says, and even though I want to ask him why he hasn't messaged me, I don't.

Instead I ask, "Do you want to be my guinea pig and let me make you a coffee? I kind of need the practice."

"Sure." He walks toward the counter, and I head behind it, where Katie and Tony are both watching me with curious looks.

"Give me your most complicated drink," I tell him, peeking my head around the espresso machine, which is taller than I am.

"I normally just drink plain coffee with cream, so you make me something you think I might like."

"Make him a flat white with cream and vanilla syrup," Katie suggests.

"Do you like vanilla?" I ask him.

"Caramel is more my thing," he says, and I swear his eyes flash to my hair, but I'm probably just imagining it.

"A flat white with caramel coming right up." I peek around to him again as I pour the milk into the steam cup. "So why are you in town?"

"Running some errands." He leans his hip against the counter and doesn't say more, so I don't either. As the espresso machine whirls and hisses, I can feel him watching me but refuse to give into checking him out. Whatever his reason for checking in on me is, it's not because he likes me as anything more than a friend. Maybe he feels sorry for me, or maybe, like he said, he knows what it's like to be somewhere new and not really have anyone.

When his drink is done, I put a lid on it and hand it over to him; then I hold my breath as he takes a sip. "So?"

"It's good." He gives me a small smile. "How much do I owe you for this?"

"It's on me." I wave him off when he starts to pull out his wallet.

"Thanks."

"No problem," I tell him, then look to the door when it opens and watch a group of people walk in.

"I'll let you get back to work." He dips his chin ever so slightly. "See you around."

"See you around." I move out of the way so that Katie can get back in front of the register but catch him reaching into his pocket, pulling out some cash, and shoving it into the tip jar before he leaves, taking his coffee with him. When he's gone, I let out a long breath.

"So is he not your boyfriend because you don't want him to be? Or is he not your boyfriend because he's a guy and they tend to be stupid?" Katie asks after we get the new group of people their drinks, and I shrug.

"Neither. He's just a friend."

"I saw the way he was watching you before you knew that he was in the store, and I can tell you that it was not the way a friend looks at another friend." It's on the tip of my tongue to ask how he was looking at me, but I refuse to do that to myself: get my hopes up and make things between us out to be more than they actually are.

"You didn't respond to his text, so he came to check on you. As a dude, I'm telling you that means he likes you," Tony says, leaning against the counter.

"Well, as much as I appreciate both of your concern about the status of Maverick's feelings for me, I'm telling you that he's just a friend. His best friend is my best friend's husband, and since I just moved to town, he's looking out for me."

"Right, keep telling yourself that," Katie says, going back to the counter when another group of customers comes in.

Thankfully the conversation about Maverick ends there, and neither she nor Tony brings him up again for the rest of the evening. That doesn't mean I don't replay in my mind each time I've been in his presence over and over again, trying to gain some kind of insight into his brain and what he's thinking.

Chapter 8

JADE

Hearing sirens behind me, I glance into my rearview mirror, then look down at my speedometer. The last speed sign I saw said that the speed limit was forty-five, so if I didn't miss one, the cop currently flagging me down to pull over isn't doing it because of that.

I slow down my car and pull onto the side of the road, putting the engine in park before I reach over into the glove box to get my registration and insurance card. As I straighten in my seat, I watch a tall, fit man in a formfitting uniform get out of his car and put a large, cream-colored cowboy hat on to cover his blond hair. I watch him get closer, then wait until he's at my window to roll it down a couple of inches.

"I wasn't speeding, was I? The last sign I saw said the limit was forty-five," I say, looking up at him, and I know that he's good looking even if I can't see his eyes, which are covered by a pair of silver aviators.

"You were driving too slow."

"What?" I frown at him, sure that I heard him wrong.

"The speed limit is sixty-five; it turned sixty-five about five miles back. Did you notice everyone passing you?"

"You're pulling me over because I was going too slow?" I can't wrap my mind around that. I've never heard of such a thing in my life.

"Yes, ma'am."

"Is this a prank?" I look behind me to see if there's cameras or something. I mean, who the heck gets pulled over for going too slow?

"It's not a prank. Just like speeding, driving too slow is dangerous."

"Yeah, I mean, I've totally seen a million signs that say, *Drive faster because driving too slow kills people*." I shake my head in disbelief. "Are you going to give me a ticket?"

"I'm going to run your license."

"Great." I pass my stuff over to him, then take off my sunglasses and rub the bridge of my nose. "How much is a ticket for going too slow?"

"I didn't say I was giving you a ticket; I just need to run your license."

"Of course, you've got to make sure I don't have any outstanding turtle tickets," I grumble, and he laughs. "I'm so glad that I amuse you."

"Me too," he says before tapping the roof of my car. "I'll be right back. Stay put."

"Oh, I will, and even if I didn't, you'd be able to catch me again," I say, listening to him chuckle as he walks off.

Sighing, I grab my cell phone from my bag and type up a quick message to Cybil, letting her know what's going on so that she doesn't show up at my place when I'm not there. Tonight, she and I are having the girls who will potentially be selling stuff out of our store over. Our goal is to find out more information about them and go over what we will be expecting and what they will get in return. The time is running out for us to make our decision, since Everly's father officially moved out of his office today.

The good news is he agreed to give us until the weekend to figure out if we want to take over the lease of the space. The bad news is we only have until the weekend. I'm nervous, much more nervous than Cybil is, because I know how it feels to have something you worked so hard for fail, and I don't know that I want to go through that again. Plus, it's not my money on the line this time; it's hers.

"You're good to go." A deep voice startles me, and I turn to face the officer, then accept my stuff back when he passes it through the window. "Just make sure that you're paying attention to the road signs from now on."

"I will, and thank you for not giving me a ticket." I tuck my license back in my wallet, then notice a piece of paper with the name Ken on it along with a phone number.

"Call if you want to grab dinner or a drink sometime," he says, and I turn in time to watch him as he takes off his shades. Darn, I was right—he is really good looking. Not as good looking as Maverick but still really good looking. "Have a good evening, Ms. Thurman."

He does the whole tap-to-the-roof-of-my-car thing again, then walks off back to his squad car. I watch him go, then tuck his number into my bag because maybe I will get a drink or dinner with him. I mean, it's probably smarter to go out with a guy who I know is interested than it is to spend my time thinking about a man who leaves me feeling confused. After I get my stuff sorted, I carefully pull back onto the road, and Officer Ken follows as I speed up; then he turns around on one of the dirt roads between the highways and heads back in the opposite direction.

I get to my house about fifteen minutes later and take the stuff I picked up from the store inside with me and dump it on the counter. Cybil and I agreed that we would have everyone over to my place—that way Tanner could stay home with Claire, and she would be in her space and hopefully give Cybil a much-needed break.

"Knock knock," Cybil calls, walking inside carrying a box that I know contains the trays and wineglasses we are going to use tonight.

"Don't you look hot." I smile at her, and she does a little shimmy.

"I haven't had a reason to wear makeup in forever, so I figured, why not do it up big."

"I'm surprised that Tanner let you leave the house looking like you do right now."

"He didn't want me to leave, but he knows I'm coming home and doing that after a couple glasses of wine." She takes the trays and glasses out of the box and sets them on the counter.

"He's a smart guy."

"He is." She comes over to where I'm taking the meat, cheese, crackers, and veggie tray out of the bags.

"Did you get my message about being pulled over?" I ask her while she opens the veggie tray, takes one of the baby carrots out, and eats it.

"No, you got pulled over? I didn't even check my phone when I picked it up to come over here."

"I did."

"Why?"

"For going too slow," I say, and she blinks at me. "I know, right? I couldn't believe it either. I mean, who gets pulled over for going too slow."

"I didn't even know that was a thing."

"I didn't know, either, but apparently it is." I take one of the trays and start laying out the cheese, crackers, and meat in rows.

"Did you get a ticket?"

"No, but I did get a number."

"Shut up. The cop that pulled you over gave you his number?" She laughs, letting her head fall back on her shoulders.

"He did."

"Was he good looking?" she asks, wiggling her brows.

"He was." I leave out that Maverick is better looking, since she doesn't even know that I have a weird one-sided crush on the guy.

"Are you going to call him?"

"I don't know, maybe. I haven't really decided." I shrug, setting the tray aside and going to grab a cutting board. "You know I have the worst luck when it comes to men, and I'm kind of enjoying my drama-free life right now."

"Not all guys are assholes." She leans into me. "I think that you should call him. I mean, if nothing else, you could use a night out. Also he did pull you over, so that means he has a job."

"I guess there really always is a positive," I say, then hear her phone ring. "That's probably Tanner asking if you're drunk yet and ready to come home." I laugh as she puts it to her ear.

"Hey, honey," she says, then laughs. "No, we don't want pizza. We are being fancy tonight and eating finger foods." She shakes her head. "Okay, well, tell him hi, and I'll see you in a bit. Oh, wait." She stops him before he can hang up. "Can you believe that Jade got pulled over for driving too slow?" She pauses. "I know, right, but the funniest part is the officer gave her his number." She laughs. "Right? So crazy. Okay, I love you. Kiss Claire for me and tell her I will be home soon." She hangs up, then takes her cell to the counter and sets it down. "Mav and Tanner are ordering pizza and wanted to see if we wanted some."

"Mav is there?" My heart does a little flutter. The stupid thing really doesn't know any better.

"He is," she says while gathering the bottles of wine and placing them on the counter. "He's been around a lot more lately, which is nice. I know Tanner was worried about him for a while; really we all kind of were."

"Why?" I ask, feeling way more curious than I probably should.

"He kind of pulled away from us around the time I had Claire and Blake got together with Everly." She smiles. "Personally I think he has a girlfriend that he's not telling us about for whatever reason and has been spending time with her." She shrugs. "Hopefully this new leaf he's turned over means that we will get to meet her soon."

"Hopefully," I agree, even though the thought of him having a girlfriend makes me feel nauseous.

"All right, enough about the guys." She fills two glasses with rosé and brings them over to where I'm standing. "Let's have a glass of wine and toast to tonight. Hopefully when this evening is over, we will be ready to move forward with signing off on the store."

"I will for sure toast to that." I clink my glass against hers, and we both take a sip before we finish getting everything ready.

Around forty minutes later, the girls we invited over start to arrive, and by the time they all leave three hours later, I'm a little more convinced that we need to do this.

Heather, a single mom in town, makes a living selling her handmade jewelry online, and every piece she brought with her is something I would buy for myself. Lonnie, a girl who grew up here, makes and hand paints pottery, which she also sells online, each mug, plate, and bowl going for over sixty-five dollars, which at first I thought was insane until I saw them in person and realized they really are like pieces of art that you use every day. And then Mary, an older woman who reminded me of an elegant bohemian goddess, designs hand-painted signs and plaques with cute little sayings on them, and the book ones she brought me as a gift are something I will gladly display. Not only was each woman talented in her craft, but I could tell they love what they do, and seeing that made me realize that if we go through with this, we will not just be making one of my dreams come true; we will be making that happen for them too.

Lying on my couch, where I planted myself twenty minutes ago when Cybil left to go home, I try to talk myself into getting into the shower, but that room feels really far away at the moment. I don't drink very often, so the four glasses of wine I drank have totally gone to my head. Hearing a knock on the door, I frown and lift my head off the arm of the couch to look at it. Obviously I don't have superpowers, so I can't see who it is, but that doesn't mean I don't try. When the person knocks again, I push up off the couch and attempt to walk in a straight line to the door but end up zigzagging my way across the room with Pebbles following me.

"I'm okay," I assure my pup, picking him up so that I don't end up stepping on him. I hold him against me as I open the door, and my heart does a stupid thump when I find Maverick standing outside with his hands tucked into his coat pockets. "Coming to check on me again?"

"After seeing how drunk Cybil was, I figured I should."

"You didn't have to." I keep myself planted in front of my door, making it clear that he's not invited in. "As you can see, I'm totally fine. Actually, when you knocked, I was headed to the shower."

"Do you want company?"

"In the shower?" I joke, and he licks his bottom lip, then smiles.

"I was thinking more along the lines of a movie." He reaches his hand out to pet the top of Pebbles's head.

"I'm just going to go to bed."

"Do you work tomorrow?"

"No." I lean into the doorjamb because standing upright is not working for me any longer. "I have the day off, so I'm spending the day in bed with a hot Russian mobster."

"A what?"

"A Russian mobster." I wave my hand out when he gives me a *What the heck are you talking about* look. "It's a book I'm reading. Do you like to read?"

"The only stuff I read is for work, so no, not really."

"That's a bummer. Tanner reads to Cybil, in the bath. It's sweet." My eyes widen when I realize what I just said. "You can't tell him that I told you about that."

"I won't," he says with a smile as a gust of wind causes me to shiver. "Go on in. It's cold out here."

"Yeah." I take a step back. "You really don't have to keep checking on me," I say, and he looks like he wants to say something but thinks better of it.

"Night, Jade."

"Night, Maverick." I watch him walk to his truck before I shut the door, then wait to hear his engine start up before I head back into my apartment.

Lying in my bed a while later after my shower, I stare at the ceiling for a long time, thinking about Maverick and what Cybil said about him pulling away from everyone. I don't think she's right about him having a girlfriend; I can't imagine him not bringing someone he cares about around to meet the people he considers his family. I wonder, though, if seeing his friends happy and falling in love didn't cause him to pull away.

And if it did, I can understand why. It's not easy watching the people you are closest to fall in love, get married, and have kids when you're still doing the same thing you were doing five years ago. So maybe his interest in me is because he knows that he and I are in the same boat, and maybe, just maybe, he needs a friend too.

JADE

After knocking on the front door of Cybil's house, I walk inside and call out, "Hello?"

"In the kitchen," Cybil calls back, so I drop my purse on the entryway table and head that way as she shouts, "Are you hungover?"

"No," I say as I find her in the kitchen helping Claire eat some kind of orange goo. "I drank about a gallon of water before I went to bed and took an aspirin." I kiss her cheek, then lean down to get a gooey kiss from Claire that tastes like orange and banana. "Are you hungover?"

"No, I thought I would be, but I woke up this morning feeling fabulous."

"Fabulous, huh?" I laugh, wiggling my brows, and she shrugs while her cheeks turn pink.

"It was a really good night."

"Good." I take a seat and rest my arms on the counter. "So what do you think about last night, and not the part that happened after you came home?"

"I'm even more convinced that we should open the store." Her gaze locks with mine. "I know you've had a lot of doubts about it, but I think that between the women we met last night, along with you and me, the store will be a success. They're going to do everything they can to get people in the store, and I know we'll do the same."

"I was thinking the same thing."

"Yeah?" she asks, her eyes lighting up.

"Yeah, even as scared as I am, I know I'll regret it if we don't do this."

"So we can call Gene and tell him that we're ready to take over the lease?" she asks, sounding excited.

"Yes," I say, and she squeals as she starts to jump around, making Claire giggle.

"I'm so darn excited. This is going to be amazing."

"I think it is too," I agree, ignoring the worry in the center of my chest because I know in my gut this is the right thing, even if it is really scary to think about failing again.

"As soon as I get Claire cleaned up, I'll call Gene and tell him the good news."

"What's the good news?" Tanner asks, coming into the kitchen.

"We just agreed to open the shop," she tells him, and with one look from him, I can tell just how proud he is of his wife and how excited he is for her. God, I love that for her, but I really want that for myself too. Someone to share things big and small with, someone to look at me like he looks at her.

"That's great news, Sunshine." He gives her a kiss, then looks at me. "I'm happy for you both."

"You might not be so happy when your wife tells you about all the work she has planned for you to do there."

"The guys and I have a lot of free time right now. It will give us something to do," he says easily, and I laugh. Of course he doesn't have an issue with doing anything his wife needs. Really, sometimes I wonder what planet Tanner is from, because he is so different from most men I know. I couldn't even get my ex to help me clean up after I cooked dinner, and I wasn't even asking him to do it all himself.

"We also need to figure out how to get all of your books and stuff here from your store sooner than later," she says, talking about all the stuff I had in my shop minus the toys I kept in the back room, since I sold those off online so that I would have a little money to hold me over while I settled in here.

"I'm sure if I call Dad, he would drive all my stuff up here if I asked him to. And you know Mom wouldn't complain about coming to spend time with Claire."

"That's true." She takes Claire out of her seat and sets her on the counter while holding her so that she can wipe Claire's face. "Oh." She looks at me over her shoulder. "Did you call the guy who gave you his number?"

"No." I shake my head.

"Why not?" She hands Claire off to Tanner when she starts to reach for him.

"I don't know . . . dating seems like a lot of work right now. I just don't know that I'm ready for that."

"You don't have to date him," Tanner says, and Cybil's nose scrunches. "You could just go out for a drink. It might be good for you to meet some new people. You know, make some friends."

"I don't think the guy is looking for a friend, honey," she tells him, and he drops his gaze to hers for a moment, then looks at me.

"Right, on that note I'm going to take my daughter and watch good ol' wholesome cartoons," he mutters and walks out of the kitchen while Cybil and I share a smile.

"I still think that you should call him. I mean, the worst that could happen is you find out that you two have nothing in common and you don't see him again."

"You're not going to drop this, are you?"

"I'm not." She comes over and leans against the counter in front of me. "I want you to find what I have." Her face goes soft. "Your person is out there somewhere, but you won't find him unless you're willing to put yourself out there again."

"You do realize that what you have is rare, right?" I ask, then add, "I've dated a lot, taken chances on men who I thought could be the one, and still have never found what you have. I love that you want me to have what you do, but I don't know that that is ever going to happen."

"Weren't you the one who told me that my Prince Charming was out there and that I would find love when I least expected it?"

"You're you. Of course I knew that you would find a guy who would sweep you off your feet and fall in love with you the moment he met you."

"You don't know how amazing you are." She pushes off the counter and comes around to me. "Your guy is out there." She wraps her arms around me. "I don't know if he's the cop who pulled you over, but I do know that you won't know that unless you give it a shot and go out with him."

"Fine, I'll call him." I give in, hugging her back, then let her go so I can stand up. "Let me get my bag." I let out a long breath.

"Yay." She grins. "I have a good feeling about this."

"At least one of us does," I grumble, hearing her laugh as I go grab my bag from where I left it. When I get back to the kitchen, I pull out Ken's number from my wallet along with my cell phone.

"You've got this," Cybil says as I plug Ken's number into my phone and press call. My stomach twists into a tight knot as the phone rings, and I'm honestly relieved when the call goes to a generic voice mail.

"Um, hey, Ken, it's Jade, the girl you pulled over for driving under the speed limit . . ." I roll my eyes at myself. God, I sound like a dork. "Call me . . . or don't." I hang up, wishing I'd thought to delete that voice mail before I'd ended the call.

"Well, okay, we might need to work on your phone skills," Cybil says, and I glare at her, then look down at my phone when it starts to ring.

Recognizing Ken's number because I just dialed it, I stare at my phone in horror as it rings again. "He's calling me back."

"Answer it." She nudges my phone, and I slide my finger across the screen on the fifth ring, then put it to my ear.

"Hello."

"I didn't think you were going to answer." Okay, so Ken also has a very nice voice, deep and rich. "I got your message."

"Yeah, sorry about that."

"It was cute," he says, then adds: "Honestly, I didn't think you'd call." *Well, I wasn't going to,* I think but don't say.

"I did . . . surprise," I say, and he laughs.

"What are you doing tonight?"

"Tonight," I repeat, and Cybil starts to nod like a madwoman. "Nothing."

"Are you up to having dinner? I get off work at six; I could meet you somewhere around seven."

"That sounds good." I drop my head in order to block out the sight of my best friend dancing around waving her arms in the air. "Do you know where you want to meet?"

"Do you like Italian?"

"I do."

"There's a great Italian place on Main Street, Amico's. We could meet there."

"Sounds good."

"I'll see you there at seven," he says, and I nod, then remember that he can't see me.

"It's a date," I say, and he laughs before saying, "Later," and hanging up.

"Wow, he must really like you if he wants to see you tonight." Cybil claps, and I put my cell phone back into my bag, wondering what the heck it is I'm doing. I have no desire to go out on a date with Ken, even as handsome as he is. "I have a really good feeling about this."

"You already said that."

"Don't be such a Debbie Downer. It's going to be awesome, plus you said it yourself that this guy is good looking, so even if he can't hold conversation and is a total drag, you'll have something pretty to look at this evening."

"There is always a positive."

"Always." She grins. "Now where are you meeting him?"

"Amico's." I shrug. "He said it's an Italian place in town."

"It's not just an Italian place; it's a really nice Italian place." She looks at her watch. "We need to go figure out what you are going to wear. Claire will be down for a nap soon. We can go down to your place once she's asleep and go through your stuff. Did you bring any dresses with you?"

"I'm not wearing a dress to dinner." I wave her off, and she pouts out her bottom lip. "You and I both know that dressing up here consists of wearing a nice sweater and your darkest blue jeans and maybe heels, if you're that kind of girl, but not a fancy dress."

"Fine." She gives in because she knows I'm right. "We won't look for a dress, but we will find you the perfect outfit for tonight."

"Sounds like fun," I lie, because all I really wanted to do today was spend some time with my friend, then go back to my place, get on my pajamas, and lie in bed with a book for the rest of the day.

"Also we need to talk about a name for the shop. I was thinking the Second Chapter, but I'm totally open to something else."

"I love that name." I feel my throat get tight. "It's perfect."

"Don't start crying, 'cause if you do, I'm going to start crying."

"I'm not going to cry." I get up and walk to where she is and wrap my arms around her. "I love you."

"Always," she whispers back. As much as I know she doesn't want it, I hope one day I can pay her back for giving me a second shot at my dream.

Chapter 10

JADE

I pull into the parking lot behind Amico's, and it takes me a minute to find a spot, since the entire lot is jam packed with cars. After putting my car in park, I flip down my visor and check my lipstick. With my makeup light, I decided to go with a red lip to add a little bit of pop, but a red lip requires some extra attention, since it has a tendency to transfer to your teeth if you're not careful.

After making sure that I'm all set, I get out of my car and tie the belt of my knee-length beige coat around my waist, which covers up all but the neck of the cream turtleneck sweater I'm wearing but allows a glimpse of my bell-bottom jeans and spike bootees. With my bag—one of Cybil's creations—slung over my shoulder, I head across the pavement toward the street since the front of the restaurant is directly on the main road.

I'm not really feeling nervous about this evening but definitely feeling unsure. Ken didn't message me again after we spoke, so I'm not sure that he's actually going to be here to meet me, and wouldn't that just be my luck, to get stood up for a date I didn't even really want to go on.

When I reach the sidewalk, I walk around the corner and come to a dead stop when I see Maverick near the entrance to the restaurant, talking to none other than Ken. Both men standing together is like a punch to the gut, and they couldn't be more opposite if they tried. Maverick is all dark hair, with striking, elegant features and warm, almond-toned skin, a contrast to Ken's stereotypically all-American features. Really the only thing the two of them have in common is they are both about the same height.

Like Maverick senses me, his head turns my direction, and his eyes sweep over me before they lock with mine. I don't know what the look he gives me means, but I do feel the way my body reacts to it.

"Jade," Ken calls, and reluctantly I pull my eyes off Maverick's and plaster a smile on my face as I force my feet to move.

"Hey." I lean up as Ken's hand curves around my waist and accept his kiss on my cheek, almost overpowered by the smell of his cologne.

"You look beautiful."

"Thank you." I lean back and try not to search for Maverick but still do, and that's when I notice he's with a woman and his attention is solely focused on her. Maybe I was wrong about him having a girlfriend; maybe Cybil was right that he wasn't ready to bring her around.

"Are you hungry?" Ken asks, and I shake off the disappointment I'm feeling and focus on him. "They said our table would be ready in a couple minutes. That was a few minutes ago."

"Awesome," I say even as my stomach roils.

"Good." He takes my elbow, his touch feeling all wrong as he walks me to the door and opens it for me. When we get inside, he gives the girl standing behind a short podium his name, and then I follow the two of them through the dark restaurant to a curved booth with a single candle lit in the middle of the table. Like a gentleman, he stands aside for me to sit before he does, then takes a seat close but not too close.

Absently I listen to the girl who sat us talk as she passes us our menus, but really my attention is across the room, where Maverick is walking toward the bar with the woman he's with. The two of them smiling at each other, the familiarity between them obvious even with the space between us. Like he can feel me watching him, his eyes come to me, then move to the man sitting next to me and fill with what I swear is jealousy.

"Do you want a glass of wine or something else?" Ken asks, grabbing my attention by placing his hand over mine, and I pull it away and place my hands in my lap.

"I would love a glass of merlot." I smile at him, then look at the woman standing next to the table, catching her smile. Wow, I was really spaced out; I didn't even notice that the woman who'd sat us had left and our waitress had come to the table.

"While I get your drinks, you two look over the menu," she says, then wanders away, stopping at a few tables before going to the bar.

With no choice I focus on the man I'm on a date with and wish I hadn't let my friend bully me into going out tonight. "So you had work today?" I ask Ken to break the ice, and he leans back in the booth and rests his hand along the back, his fingers way too close to my shoulder.

"I did. I wish I had weekends off, but I work most of them, especially with overtime."

"That has to be hard."

"It is, but I love my job."

"That's always a good thing," I say, then thank my lucky stars when our waitress appears with a glass of wine for me and a tumbler half-filled with ice and some dark liquid for him.

"So tell me about yourself," he says when the waitress walks away, and I take a sip of wine before I set my glass down and meet his gaze. As much as I don't want to do this, the whole small-talk-and-find-out-about-each-other business, I know that I need to do what Cybil said and try because who knows: this guy could be my perfect match.

"I just moved here from Oregon a couple of weeks ago."

"Really? I love Oregon; it's beautiful there."

"It is."

"So what brought you to Montana?"

"My best friend, who is like my sister, moved here a while ago after she met her husband."

"So you moved to be closer to her?"

"No." I take another sip of wine. "I moved here because my life back home kind of imploded. I had a bookstore, and it went under, and then the guy I was seeing screwed me over, so it was either stay there and try to start over or do the starting over somewhere else." I spit it all out, which isn't something I would normally do, but then again, I might as well get it over with from now so he knows what a mess my life has been.

"Sorry."

"Stuff happens, right?"

"Right," he agrees softly, then adds, "I think everything happens for a reason, so you're right where you're supposed to be."

"That's a good way to look at life," I tell him with a smile, feeling myself relax as the wine starts to warm my stomach.

"Have you two decided what you want to order?" our waitress asks, coming up to the table. I look at the menu in front of me, realizing that I haven't even touched it.

"I'm ready if you are," Ken says, so I nod, figuring that we are at an Italian restaurant, so spaghetti has to be on the menu. After giving her my order, I listen to him give her some kind of complicated dish, then watch him pull out his phone when it rings. "Sorry, it's work; I have to take it." He scoots out of the booth with his phone in his hand.

"No problem. I'll be here," I tell him, then watch him wait until he's outside the restaurant before he puts his phone to his ear.

With him gone, I look to the bar, where Maverick was sitting with his date. He's not there anymore. Refusing to let my mind wander to what he's doing, I scoot out of the booth with my bag. I should have a couple of minutes before Ken gets back, so I make my way to the restroom. After taking care of my business and washing my hands, I start walking back through the restaurant but pause when I see that

Ken is back at our table with Maverick sitting where I was just a few minutes ago.

Like any smart woman, I look from them to the door, calculating how long it would take for me to get from here to there and what the chances are that either of them will spot me if I try to run.

"Jade." At my name I turn and find the woman Maverick is here on a date with standing a couple of feet away with a wide smile on her face. God, up close she is seriously pretty.

"Umm." I feel my brows draw together because it's obvious by her smile that she thinks she knows me, but I have no idea who she is.

"Margret," she says as she points at herself. "I recognized you from all the pictures Cybil has of you and her. I'm Blake's sister." She gives me a crooked smile before stepping forward to give me a hug. "Sorry, I've heard so much about you, so I feel like I know you, even though I haven't met you until now."

"It's nice to finally meet you. Cybil loves you; she talks about you and your daughter all the time," I say as I tuck away the jealousy I feel, jealousy that has everything to do with her being here with Maverick. I mean, it would make sense that he hasn't told anyone that he's dating his friend's sister.

"I've been meaning to stop by the house to meet you, but I've been crazy busy between work and life," she says as I adjust my bag on my shoulder. "Is Cybil here?" She looks around, and I shake my head no.

"She's at home with Tanner and Claire," I tell her, then point across the room to where Ken is still sitting with Maverick. "I'm actually here on a date." I see her look the way I pointed, then watch her brows drag together for a moment before her eyes meet mine and some kind of strange look fills them.

"I was here with Maverick while I waited for my boyfriend to get off work."

"Boyfriend?" That information shouldn't fill me with as much relief as it does, but there is no denying I feel relieved that she's not dating Maverick.

"Yeah, my boyfriend, Mason, works down the street as a bartender." Her eyes light up on the word *boyfriend*. "Mav told me that he was going to be in town and asked if I wanted to get a drink before I went to meet Mason. You know Maverick, right?"

"I do." I don't elaborate.

"And apparently he knows your date," she says after glancing that way once more, and I turn to find Maverick and Ken laughing about something.

"Apparently," I mutter. Then next thing I know, her fingers are wrapped around my wrist, and she is towing me with her across the restaurant. When we reach the table, I fight the urge to shift on my heels as both guys turn their attention to us.

"Sorry to interrupt, boys," she says before she basically forces me to sit down on the side of the booth next to Ken, then scoots in next to me. "Jade was just telling me that she was here on a date with you." She looks at Ken. "And I thought, *Wow, that's insane,* because I'm here on a date with Mav." She motions to the guy across the table from her. The man who is currently scowling at her. "It's a small world, right?" She nudges my shoulder, completely ignoring Maverick's look.

"Really small," I agree, wondering what she is up to but seeing that it's something even after knowing her for just a couple of minutes.

"You don't mind if we join you guys, right?" she asks Ken, and I peek over at him, seeing that he's not exactly happy with the idea of company.

"Of course not." He wraps his arm around my shoulder, and I squirm when I notice Maverick's jaw clench.

"Yay." Margret drags me away from Ken and pulls me into her side, which forces him to let me go. "Did you guys order dinner yet?"

"We did." I reach across the table for my wine because if wine were ever a necessity, it would be in this exact moment.

"We haven't yet." She looks across the table to where Maverick is sitting. "Do you know what you want to eat, sweetie?"

"I'm not hungry," he answers with a tone filled with annoyance.

"Of course you're hungry; why else would you ask me to meet you at a restaurant? Especially when I suggested we just meet at the bar down the street for a drink." She laughs. "You were pretty insistent that we come here; I can only assume that's because you were hungry for Italian." My eyes fly to Maverick's, and my skin prickles as our gazes lock. He knew I was going to be here. I don't know how he knew, but he did. My heart starts to pound so hard I wonder if you can't see the pulse in my neck.

"Shit," Ken curses, and I force my attention off Maverick to look at my date, sure that he knows something is up. But when I turn toward him, I see his attention is across the room, and I turn to see what has caught his attention and find a blonde with big hair, lots of cleavage, and a murderous look on her face coming our way.

"This is you working late?" the blonde yells, coming toward us and pointing a finger at Ken. "I knew it. I fucking knew it." Her voice rises as her face starts to get red. "You're a fucking liar."

"Oh my God," I breathe, spinning my head around toward Ken, who looks like he wants to bolt but is trapped. "You have a girlfriend?"

"No, bitch, he has a fucking wife," the woman yells, sounding closer than she was seconds ago, and I find her right at the edge of the table glaring at me while holding out her hand, which is sporting a good-size diamond.

"I didn't know," I tell her, noticing that the room has gone quiet and everyone is now watching us.

"Right, that's what they all say. *I didn't know.*" She uses a fake baby voice. "Give me a fucking break."

"I met him yesterday; we had one phone call. I had no idea he had a wife. I don't know anything about him."

"You don't have to explain yourself," Maverick cuts in, and I wish the ground would open up and swallow me. How the hell is my luck this bad—of course Maverick is here to witness exactly how horrible I am at choosing men.

"She does need to explain herself, and she also needs to tell me where the fuck she met my husband."

"Donna, let's talk about this outside," Ken says as Maverick lets him out of the booth on his side.

"That's a great idea," Margret agrees. "You two take your drama outside."

"Bitch, who the fuck are you?" Donna asks on a hiss, leaning in toward Margret.

"Lower your tone, stop tossing around the word *bitch*, and take your husband and marital problems somewhere else," Margret says, starting to get up, and I grab the back of her shirt to keep her seated.

"Let's go. We'll talk." Ken grabs Donna's arm, or tries to, but she yanks it out of his grasp and spins around, shoving him in the chest hard enough that he is forced a step back.

"Do not touch me." She shoves him again, then throws her arms down at her sides and gets up on her tiptoes so that she can yell in his face. "I want a divorce. I'm tired of this." Her voice cracks, and my heart breaks for her because I know how she's feeling. Know what that kind of pain feels like. "You keep doing this to me over and over, and I keep taking you back like an idiot."

"Baby, I love you," Ken tells her on a sigh.

"That's a lie," Margret mumbles, and I elbow her.

"You love yourself; you don't love me. I don't even think you care about me," Donna says, sounding broken.

"Of course I love you and care about you."

"If you did, you wouldn't be able to hurt me like you do," she whispers with tears now falling quickly from between her lashes. "I can't do this anymore."

"We'll go home and talk." Ken tries to grab her, but she shakes her head and takes another step back away from him.

"No, I'm not going home. I'm going to my parents', and tomorrow while you're at work, I'll get all my stuff."

"You can't leave me."

"I can and I am going to." She wipes the tears away. "I'm done."

"You don't even have a job. You won't be able to survive without me," he tells her, and I can see that statement's made an impact. Dick.

"You can work with me," I blurt when I notice her start to waver, and she looks at me and blinks. "My best friend and I are opening a store in town; we'll hire you once we open."

"Jesus," Maverick mutters, but I ignore him and keep my attention on her.

"Or I work at the Bear now. I could probably get you a job there," I tell her, then add stupidly: "The tips are pretty good."

She stares at me for a moment, and I'm half-ready for her to ask me if I'm on something, but she doesn't; instead she looks up at her husband. "See, I can get a job. I don't need you." She looks back at me and swallows. "Thank you."

"You're welcome," I whisper. Then with that, she spins on her heel and heads out of the restaurant with Ken hot on her tail.

"I really hope she doesn't take that douche back," Margret says as they walk outside and the chatter in the restaurant begins to resume.

"I hope not too." I scrub my fingers through my hair. "I can't believe that he had a wife."

"How could you know?" Margret wraps her arm around my shoulders.

"I could have asked."

"Do you really think that he would have told you that he was married?" She laughs. "That's doubtful, and he didn't have on a ring or even a tan line from wearing one, so there was literally no way for you to know that he is married without him being honest, and it's obvious that he's not a very honest guy."

"You're right." I then sigh when our waitress comes to the table with the food we ordered. "I'm so sorry about this, but do you mind boxing that up for me?"

"Of course not." She gives me a solemn smile. "Do you need anything else?"

"Yes, the check please." I laugh because it's either do that or cry. I mean, not only did I just experience the worst date of my life, which is saying something since I've had some real doozies, but now I get to pay for it too.

"I'll be right back." She walks away, carrying the food. I ignore everyone in the restaurant I can feel glancing over at me and avoid making eye contact with Maverick, even though I can feel his gaze on me like a physical caress. I grab my bag so that I can get my wallet. The sooner that I get this all paid for, the sooner I can get out of here and go home. If it weren't so late, I would stop by Cybil's and tell her what happened and make sure she knows that I'm never letting her talk me into going on a date again.

"Jade," Maverick says softly.

"Yep." I don't look at him; instead I pull out my credit cards, trying to remember how much money I have on each one. Before I lost my business, I would try to keep my cards paid off or down to at least half my credit limit at all times, but I've been using them a lot more lately so that I can hold myself over until I get my first paycheck from the coffee shop. Now I will probably have to split the bill among a few different cards.

"Jade, look at me."

"Just a second." My eyes fill with tears. God, I do not want to cry right now, but this just keeps getting worse.

"Jade." Margret rests her hand on my back.

"I'm okay," I assure her as I hear some shuffling. Then I'm turned, arms wrap around me, and I'm held against a warm, hard chest.

"You're not paying for this fucking meal," Maverick growls, and I feel like an idiot when I can't stop the tears that begin to fall from my eyes. "And please stop crying unless you want me to go track down that guy and kill him."

"I'm not crying," I lie, bringing my hand up between us and using the sleeve of my sweater to wipe away my tears.

"Let me look at you." He wraps his fingers around my lower jaw, then pulls up, giving me no choice but to meet his gaze. "No more tears." He uses his thumb to swipe under my eyes, and I let out a long breath, then put some space between us, because even if I really like the way it feels being so close to him, I know that I shouldn't.

"We should all go to the bar and have a drink," Margret says, and I turn toward her.

"Thank you for the offer, but I think I'm just going to go home. I would love to get together another time, though."

"We'll plan it, and maybe Everly and Cybil can join us. We'll have a girls' night; the guys can all hang out and watch the kids."

"I would love that," I tell her, then look at the waitress when she comes back to the table carrying a plastic bag.

"Your check was taken care of," she tells me, and I blink at her. "The guy who you were here with called in and paid for it."

"Good to know he's not a complete scumbag," Margret mutters, scooting out of the booth.

"Did he leave you a tip?" I ask her as I stand and put on my coat.

"He did," she assures me, then smiles, handing me the food, which I take with a quiet thank-you before I walk through the restaurant, feeling Maverick's hand warm against my lower back and the heat from everyone watching us.

When we get outside, I look between Margret and Maverick, then hold out the bag of food. "I won't eat this. Do either of you want it? I don't want to throw it out."

"I'll take it." Margret takes it from me with a soft look. "Mason will be happy to have something to eat when he gets off work."

I pull my jacket tighter around me, then lift my bag up on my shoulder. "It was nice meeting you."

"You too." She leans in to give me a hug. "And if you need anything, get my number from Cybil."

"I will." I pull back, then look at Maverick, noticing his jaw is clenched. "See you around?" I ask, and he lifts his chin. "Cool." I lift my hand and wiggle my fingers. "Have a good night, guys." I turn and walk down the sidewalk, ignoring the sound of footsteps behind me.

"Jade," Maverick calls when I've almost reached my car, and I start to dig in my bag for my key.

"Yeah."

"Jade."

"What?" I turn, and next thing I know, he's in my space, his hand is wrapped around the back of my head, and he's leaning into me, covering my mouth with his. The kiss feels almost punishing at first; then his tongue slides across my bottom lip. Instinctively my lips part, and his tongue slides across mine. I lift my hand to his side to hold on, and his fingers in my hair tighten. I've never been kissed like he's kissing me, like he can't get enough. I whimper, overwhelmed, and he growls in return, then rips his mouth away but keeps his face close to mine.

"Fuck, I knew that would happen," he whispers, squeezing his eyes closed.

"What?" I whisper back with my heart pounding and my lips and scalp tingling.

"I knew that if I gave in to the urge I had to kiss you, that I would want to kiss you again," he says, sounding pissed, and I stare at him, not sure how to respond. "I don't feel right leaving Margret alone, so I'm going to walk her over to the bar, and once I know she's good with Mason, I'll head to your place."

"Maverick." I shake my head, not sure that that's smart, and he gets closer, which seems impossible since we are pressed chest to chest.

"I'll be thirty minutes behind you." His eyes drop to my mouth, and his thumb skims across my bottom lip before he lets me go and steps back. "Get in your car."

I do without a word. I hurry up and get into my car, then start the engine and back out of my spot, feeling his eyes on me the entire time.

Chapter 11

JADE

Sitting in the parking lot of one of the burger places in town, I dip my hot fries into my vanilla shake, then shove them into my mouth. I was halfway to my house when I got over the fact that Maverick had kissed me, and I realized there was no way I could go home, so I turned around and went back to town, where I drove around for a bit before deciding to get something to eat.

As much as I enjoyed the kiss Maverick and I shared, and as much as I want to kiss him again, I can't go there. My track record with men is not good—case in point tonight—and there is no way I want to risk making things awkward. And they would be at some point; it's inevitable with my luck.

When my phone rings, I expect it to be Maverick calling me again, but Cybil's number pops up on my dash. I want to ignore it but don't want her worried about me. I'm sure she's curious about how my date went.

"Hey," I answer after I press the button on my steering wheel.

"Where are you? I walked down to your place to see how dinner went, but you weren't there."

"Sorry, I'm parked outside of Jane's Burgers eating my feelings," I tell her, picking up my soda.

"You're what? Why?"

"Ken is married." I set down my drink and grab my burger. "His wife showed up while we were waiting for our food to arrive."

"Shut up. You're lying."

"Oh, I wish I was, but unfortunately I'm not." I shove some more fries into my mouth and chew. "And if you don't believe me, there are about a hundred people who witnessed what happened and can vouch for me."

"I can't believe he's married," she hisses. "What a prick."

"Yeah, so needless to say, I'm officially done with anything having to do with men."

"I'm sorry, Jade. God, I feel like a jerk for insisting you call that guy."

"It's fine. Really I feel bad for his wife; it seemed like it wasn't the first time that he's cheated on her."

"Why do men do that?" she says, and I know she's shaking her head in disgust.

"I don't know." I grab a few more fries. "In other news, I did offer his wife a job."

"You what?" she yells.

"He told her that she wouldn't be able to make it without him, so I told her that she could work for us or that I could get her a job at the Bear."

"Of course you did." She laughs. "God, I love you."

"I love you too."

"So you're in town eating in your car?"

"Yeah."

"Tanner said he thought he saw Maverick's truck drive down to your place earlier."

"Since he was with Margret at the restaurant and they both witnessed the whole scene, I bet he was probably coming to check on me." I bite my lip, hating that I'm keeping things from my best friend. But I know her; I know that if I tell her about the kiss, she's going to start getting ideas in her head, and I already have enough ideas of my own. "By the way, I really like Margret; she's sweet."

"She's the sweetest," she agrees, then asks: "When are you going to be home?"

"Maybe thirty minutes or so."

"Do you want me to come hang with you? Claire is asleep; I could bring some wine, and we could watch a movie or something."

"As much as I appreciate that offer, I think I'm just going to go to bed early tonight. It's been a long day, plus I didn't sleep great last night."

"Are you sure?"

"Yeah," I assure her. "Plus, tomorrow we have to meet with Gene before I start work, so I want to make sure that I'm up early for that." I remind her of the meeting we have scheduled to sign the lease.

"Okay," she says, sounding unsure. "If you change your mind, you know I'm just a phone call away."

"I know. Love you."

"Love you, too, and I'll see you in the morning."

"See you in the morning." I hang up after she says goodbye, then finish my food before I dump my garbage in one of the trash bins near the restaurant.

When I get home a while later, I head inside and change into a pair of sleep shorts and a tank top, then make myself a cup of tea before I get comfortable on the couch with the book I've been reading and my favorite blanket.

"Jade." Fingers slide down the side of my face, and I blink my eyes open, sure I'm dreaming when I come face-to-face with Maverick.

"What are you doing here?" I sit up, knocking the book I was reading off my lap.

"I told you I was stopping by." He picks the book up and looks at the cover, shaking his head before handing it to me.

"How did you get in here?" I look at the door, which I'm sure I locked, then glance around for Pebbles, who was with me earlier, and spot him in his bed next to the TV, still asleep. Obviously he's the worst guard dog ever.

"Picked the lock when you didn't answer." He shrugs like it's no big deal and it's not breaking and entering.

"You broke into my house."

"I didn't break in; I just used a different method to gain entry." He takes a seat next to me. "You weren't here when I stopped by earlier."

"I went to get something to eat," I tell him because there is no way I'm telling him I was hiding even if that's what I was doing. He watches me as I pull my legs up and wrap my arms around my shins, then smiles.

"I think we both know you were trying to avoid me."

"Yeah, right," I scoff. "Why would I need to avoid you?"

"Because you like kissing me as much as I like kissing you. And that scares the shit out of you." He touches my fingers. "I get it," he says quietly. "Why do you think I've been trying to keep my distance?"

"Is that why you've been showing up wherever I am?"

"I didn't say I was good at staying away from you." Oh God, it shouldn't make me happy to hear him admit that he can't stay away from me.

"How did you know where I was going to be tonight?" I fiddle with the edge of my blanket.

"Tanner mentioned it when I talked to him on the phone."

"So you decided to ask Margret to meet you there."

"Figured it would look a lot less odd if I was there with someone else." His expression becomes serious. "I didn't like the idea of you going out on a date."

"You didn't?"

"Not even a little."

"Well, if it makes you feel better, I didn't want to go out with Ken, and I didn't like that you were there with Margret before I knew who she was," I tell him, and we both get quiet and just stare at each other for a long moment before he asks: "So what do we do about this?"

"I don't know." I lift one shoulder ever so slightly. "Ignore it."

"Ignore it." His lips twitch. "I think you get that that's not happening. I want you. Even now it's taking all my control not to kiss you again," he says, and my scalp tingles while my stomach dips.

"You're best friends with Tanner and close to Cybil. I don't want things to get weird."

"Right," he says, not looking happy. "We keep it between us for the time being."

I lick my lips. Could I do that? I eye him, not sure that's any smarter than being with him and people knowing. *I* would still know, and since I already like him, I can see myself falling for him quickly, probably too quickly. On the other hand, I have a feeling that even if I didn't agree to this, it would still happen anyway. The attraction is just too strong to deny.

"Whatever happens, we remain friends or at least friendly." I hold out my pinkie, and he drops his gaze to my hand and wraps his finger around mine.

"Do you work tomorrow?" he asks, keeping my finger trapped by his.

"Yeah, and Cybil and I are supposed to meet with Gene in the morning to sign the papers for the lease."

"Do you have plans tomorrow evening?"

"No." I shake my head.

"I'll make us dinner at my place."

"Okay." Nervous anticipation causes my pulse to kick up a notch, and he leans into me. I expect him to kiss me; instead his lips brush across my forehead.

"I'll text you my address." He lets my finger go and stands.

"I'll walk you out." I get off the couch, trying not to be disappointed that I didn't get another kiss. "Come on, Pebbles," I call, figuring now is as good of a time as any to take him out for the last time tonight. "Do you need to go outside?" I pick him up when he hops up on my leg, then grab his new leash, a retractable one that allows him room to go out and potty and me to stay inside where it's warm. I hook it to his collar as we head through Cybil's shop.

"You need a robe," Maverick says when he opens the door, and I look up to find his eyes on my chest, the cold air having caused my nipples to tighten.

"He's quick, so I normally don't have to stand here long." I place Pebbles on the ground, and he runs out the door. I cross my arms over my chest and bounce on my toes, then let out a gasp when Maverick grabs my wrist and drags me against his warm chest, then folds his jacket around me.

"Better?"

"Yes," I say, quietly closing my eyes. Lord, he smells good and feels good.

"You're short." He rests his chin on the top of my head, and I tip my head back to glare at him.

"I'm not short. I'm average."

"Four foot nine is not average, babe."

"I'm five two, which is normal. You're just abnormally tall."

"Hmm." His eyes roam my face.

"How do you know Ken?"

"I don't." His hold on me tightens. "I was outside waiting for Margret to arrive, and him and I just started talking. Then you showed up."

"It seemed like you knew him. You were sitting down with him at the table like you two were best buds."

He shakes his head. "When I saw you head for the restroom and him back at the table, I decided I'd feel him out. Now I wish I would have pulled you away from him the second I saw you outside the restaurant. That's what I wanted to do."

"After what happened, I wish you would have." I let out a long breath.

"That guy was a dick."

"Yeah," I agree, then notice him looking down at my side and feel cold paws land against my calf.

"He's back." Bummer, I think, letting Maverick go and starting to take a step back, but he stops me by grasping my jaw and tipping my head back. When he dips his head and touches his mouth to mine in a soft, sweet kiss that makes my toes curl, I know I could definitely get used to him kissing me.

"I'll see you tomorrow." He pulls back to meet my eye before he lets me go.

"See you tomorrow." I pick up Pebbles so that he doesn't run out after Maverick when he walks out, then wait until he's at his truck to shut the door. I hear him drive away as I enter my place, then lock the door and let Pebbles down. After picking up my stuff, I get into bed, and I lie there for a long time, trying not to overthink things or get myself worked up about what might or might not happen. Still, it takes forever for me to find sleep.

∼

With snow beginning to fall, I turn into Maverick's driveway the next evening feeling butterflies fill my stomach. All day I've been anticipating seeing him, and he made it obvious that he was feeling the same way. Not only did he text me his address like he said he would, but he sent me a message asking what I was in the mood to eat, another asking if I wanted to have wine with dinner, and another just checking in, asking how my day was going. It was sweet and unexpected. I also really appreciated knowing that he was thinking about me as much as I was thinking about him.

As I park in front of his house next to his truck, I grab my purse from the passenger seat and get out, tucking my keys into my bag. When I start for the house, the front door opens and Maverick steps outside. His eyes roam over me from the top of my head to my feet, and surprisingly I don't feel uncomfortable, even though I worked until after six and didn't go home and change, so I'm in my jeans, sneakers, and a long-sleeved T-shirt with the coffee shop's logo on the front. Not something I would normally wear on a date.

"Hey." I walk up the steps, and he meets me halfway across the porch. "It's starting to snow."

"I see that." He leans down to kiss me like it's something he's always done, then slides my bag off my shoulder. "I didn't hear your car pull up. How was work?"

"Good, slow until after three; then we were slammed until six." I enter the house before him, and my stomach rumbles when the scent of garlic and bread fills my nose. I slip off my shoes as he places my bag on one of the hooks near the door. "Did you have a good day?"

"I had a meeting with the architect that is helping me design my house." He places his hand against my lower back and leads me to the kitchen. "He's submitting the paperwork this week to get approval so that we can hopefully break ground next year."

"That's exciting." I take a seat at the island when he pulls out a chair for me.

"How did it go with you and Cybil signing off on the space for the store?"

"Great." I watch him open a bottle of red wine. "Gene told us that we can remove the wall that's between the front room and the back, which will make the layout of the store a lot less office-like. Thank you." I accept a glass when he passes it to me, then hold it as he fills it. "So I think that tomorrow while I'm at work, Cybil is taking Tanner over there to show him what we want done exactly and then putting him to work." I grin. "Don't be surprised if you get dragged into helping him out."

"I know him, Blake, and I are going a little stir crazy having so much time on our hands, so I don't think any of us will complain about having something to do," he says easily as he grabs a bottle of beer from the fridge and opens it before he walks to the oven. My mouth waters as he grabs a pot holder and pulls out a loaf of french bread, which is open faced and buttery golden brown, and a dish that looks like pasta with cheese baked on top.

"Do you want me to help with anything?"

"Nope, just sit there and relax." He gets down plates, prepares both of them, and brings them over to where I'm sitting before he goes to the fridge and grabs a bag of salad and a couple of different types of dressing.

"What do you guys do in the off-season when you're not taking guests out on retreats?" I ask him, taking a sip of wine.

"Repair shit that needs to be fixed, work on stuff around the lodge, and take guys out on hunting trips. We keep pretty busy, but we're around a lot more, so between the three of us and Everly running the office, there's not much to do."

"Hence your willingness to help with getting the store ready." I smile at him.

"We would all find a way to get that done for you girls even if we were in the middle of the summer rush," he tells me, and my belly dips.

"This smells delicious. Thank you for cooking for me." I take a fork from him before he comes to take a seat next to me.

"Dig in, but save room for dessert; I picked up vanilla ice cream and an apple pie from the Amish market."

"Would you be pissed if I skipped dinner and just had dessert?" I ask, and he chuckles.

"No, but you don't want to miss out on the pasta. It's a favorite of my nephews', who hate almost everything," he tells me as I pick up a forkful of pasta soaked with red sauce and covered with melted cheese. I feel him watch me as I take a bite, and I barely hold back a moan of approval. "Good?"

"Better than good," I answer after I swallow. "Who taught you to cook?" I take a sip of wine, then turn to focus on him as I eat.

"My sister." His face softens. "Our dad worked three jobs, so she pretty much raised me, taught me how to cook, clean, do laundry, and work hard."

"Those are all good things to learn."

"Yeah." He picks up his beer.

"So you two are close?"

"Very, she's more like a mom to me than a sister."

"Is she much older than you?"

"She's ten years older than me, so even though I wasn't her kid, she took me on like I was. It sucked for her because she didn't have much of a childhood, since she spent most of it raising me, picking me up from school, helping me with homework, cooking me dinner, then working when she was old enough to get a job."

"That must have been hard on her."

"If you ask her if it was, she'd tell you no, but I know it must have been difficult to miss out on hanging with friends and going to things like prom or school dances because she was forced to raise her kid brother and grow up before she should have."

"You were lucky to have her."

"I was."

"And now she's in Seattle?"

"Yep, she moved there as soon as I graduated high school and joined the military. She waited until I was off doing my thing before she went to school to do hair, and now she owns a fancy salon, her husband works for a radio station, and the two of them spend all their free time trying to control Wyatt and Carter, my nephews, who are now six."

"I love that."

"Me too," he says as I take the last bite of food from my plate.

"So can you cook?"

"I should lie and say yes to try and impress you, but I feel like that might end up biting me in the ass if you ever ask me to cook something," I say, listening to him laugh as I take another sip of wine. "The truth is I can't cook; my mom tried to teach me, but I was always more interested in reading than hanging out in the kitchen with her and Cybil."

"You can make a mean cup of whatever the fuck it was that you made me the other day."

"That I can do," I agree.

"That said, you can't fucking dance," he says, and I laugh, tossing my head back. When I lower my chin, I find him watching me with a soft look; then his hand slides around the side of my neck and his fingers spear into my hair so that he can use his hold to drag me closer. His warm breath whispers across my skin, and my eyes slide closed as he kisses my jaw, the edge of my mouth, then nibbles on my bottom lip.

"Maverick." I turn on my stool, and he traps my knees between his while my hands move to his sides, my fingers wrapping around the thin shirt he has on.

"Fuck, I love the way you say my name." He rubs his lips against mine, and I chase his mouth, wanting him to kiss me more than I want my next breath.

When he does finally give me what I want, I lose myself in him, his taste, the feel of his fingers in my hair, his hand on my side, his thumb so close to my nipple. The space between my legs floods with heat and my pulse skyrockets when his hand lifts and he cups my breast.

I move closer, wanting more, and without me having to say a word, he gives me what I need by moving my knees from between his, grabbing my ass, and tugging me onto his lap. With no space between us, I circle his shoulders with my arms and thread my fingers through his hair, which is soft and thick. My core pulses as I rock against him, and

I don't remember a time I was ever turned on like I am right in this moment, and he hasn't even really touched me yet. "Are you wet?" he asks, trailing his mouth to my ear, dragging his teeth over my earlobe.

"Yes." My breath hitches when he lifts my shirt and trails his fingers around to the front of my jeans.

"How wet?"

My stomach muscles contract as he unbuttons my jeans and drags down the zipper.

"Oh fuck, soaked." He groans when his fingers make contact with my sex.

"Maverick." My hips jump when he skims over my clit.

"Gonna move us, baby. I want to touch you." He stands with me still on his lap and moves us across the room. I hold on to him as he carries me, nuzzling his neck, then brace as I fall back onto the couch and he comes down on me. He kisses me again while his hands move up the front of my shirt, and my back arches as he cups my breast over my bra.

I expect him to take off my top, but he doesn't; he trails his hand down my stomach, then works it into the front of my jeans. As his fingers part my folds, I moan against his mouth.

"So slick. I can't wait to get inside you." He works one finger and then another into me, pumping slow. "Do you want that? Me to fill you up?" He nuzzles my throat over my pulse, and my heart skips a beat.

"Oh God." My neck arches when he rolls over my clit.

"Do you know how badly I want you?" He presses the hard length of his cock into my hip while his fingers slide back inside me, making me whimper. Even through his jeans he feels huge, thick and long. "I've imagined how you taste, how that red hair of yours will look spread out on my pillow as I fuck you, the way you'll moan my name as you take me."

Okay, so I didn't know that dirty talk was something that would get me off, but as my scalp tingles, my toes curl, and my core begins to clench around his fingers, I realize it does and in a big way. Or maybe it's just him saying those things to me in his deep voice.

"I'm coming," I whisper, digging my nails into his sides as he continues to finger fuck me through my orgasm, an orgasm that feels like an out-of-body experience. Stars dance behind my closed lids, and every muscle in my body tightens, then relaxes, turning me into a pile of mush. I lie there with my eyes closed, breathing heavy and trying to come to terms with how quickly he got me off when I don't think I've ever had an orgasm with a man without me doing what I need to to get off.

"You okay?" He nuzzles my neck, carefully removing his hand from between my legs.

"I think so." I open my eyes to find him looking down at me, smiling.

"You came hard." I did, harder than I've ever come in my life, even with myself. Not that I'm going to tell him that.

"Come here." He pulls me up, then takes a seat on the couch and holds me against his chest. I close my eyes and wrap my arms around his waist, just listening to the sound of his heartbeat, feeling my eyes beginning to get heavier and heavier with every second that passes.

"Are you falling asleep on me?" he asks quietly, and I smile.

"Maybe. It was an early morning, my belly is full, and I had an amazing orgasm." I lean back to look at him, then laugh when Caz jumps up on the couch behind him and rests her paws on his shoulder to get closer to me.

"Hey, pretty girl." I pet the top of her head, hearing her purr, then hold her when she climbs into my lap.

"Cockblocked by my cat," he mutters, sounding not annoyed or frustrated but like he's joking, which is a surprise given that I can still feel how hard he is.

"Sorry," I say, letting Caz go, and she hops off the couch. "Where were we?" I lean in to kiss him, and he pulls back just an inch.

"As much as I want that, I know you gotta drive home, and the snow is getting heavier," he tells me softly, sliding his hand into the hair at the side of my head, and I look out the window and notice big white flakes falling steadily from the sky. "When is your next day off?"

"Saturday."

"Let's plan for you to stay over on Saturday then."

"You want me to stay the night?"

"Yeah," he says easily, and I wonder what planet he's from; most men are all about getting some and then having their space back.

"Cybil will probably wonder where I am," I point out quietly, and he shrugs.

"Tell her that you're staying the night with me."

"I thought we were keeping this between us for now."

"Right." He removes his hand from my hair, and his sudden change in demeanor makes my brows drag together. The twitch of his jaw and the way his body under mine has gotten tight.

"Are you mad?"

"No," he says, but I'd bet money that he is, which is something I just do not understand. I wasn't the only one who agreed to our deal. "It's getting late, and I want you to get home safe before the roads are bad."

"Sure." I get off his lap, and he stands.

"Are you going to be okay to drive?"

"I'll be fine." I go with him to the kitchen and start to pick up my plate so I can take it to the sink, but he stops me with a shake of his head.

"Leave it. I'll clean up after I walk you out."

"Are you sure?" I ask, trying to understand what is happening here.

"Yeah, just get your shoes," he tells me, heading for the front door, and I watch him go, shaking my head. After I get my bag and put on my shoes, he opens the front door for me and walks with me to my car, the energy vibrating off him, making it clear that he's not a happy camper. "Thank you again for dinner." I stop and look up at him as snowflakes dance around us. Not knowing what to do but understanding that he wants me gone, I open my door and start to get in behind the wheel but stop when he spins me around. His mouth lands on mine in a kiss that is hard and over before it even really begins.

"Call me as soon as you get home so I know you made it safe," he demands after ripping his mouth from mine, and I nod while my chest heaves. Then I allow him to help me into my seat.

As soon as I have my seat belt on, he slams my door shut, then steps back, crossing his arms over his chest, and he stays that way as I back out and pull away from his house.

While his house disappears from my rearview mirror, I'm still at a loss to understand what just transpired, but I'm not dumb enough to think that it won't happen again, especially with him refusing to explain to me what was going on in his head.

And as I drive home with the snow falling steadily, I get more and more annoyed with him for acting just like every other guy who has messed with my head. I do not need one more man who agrees with me on something big, then turns around and changes his mind because it no longer fits his prerogative. Screw that.

Chapter 12

JADE

Standing behind the counter at the Bear, I scroll through a list of new-release books and write down the ones I think might sell well in the store. With a list that is already a mile long, I wish I had an endless supply of money and space, because if it were possible, every book available for purchase would have a home on one of my shelves.

Hearing my cell phone beep on the counter, I pick it up and bite my lip when I find a text from Maverick. Last night when I got home, I called like he'd asked me to and let him know that I was safe, then quickly got off the phone. Not that he seemed to mind. Whatever had been bothering him when I'd been at his place was still obviously bothering him then. So seeing his name on my phone is a surprise, since I didn't think I'd hear from him again. I figured that he was done with me for whatever reason and I would just have to accept that things hadn't worked out. Which would probably be better for all parties involved, because when he's not acting like a jerk, I do really like him way more than I probably should at this point.

Coming out of my head when the door dings, I look up and smile when I see Tanner and Cybil walk in holding Claire.

"Did you guys already go next door?" I ask, and Cybil grins as I set my phone down without opening Maverick's message.

"We did, and good news: that wall is not load bearing, so Tanner will be able to take it out without it costing us tons of money."

"Look at you, using construction lingo." I walk around the counter so I can take my niece from her. "And that's great news." I glance up at Tanner. "What did you think of the space—do you like it?"

"It's nice. You guys will get lots of foot traffic. It's in a prime location."

"We hope so." I bounce Claire when she starts to fuss, then kiss her cheek and ask, "Do you want a cookie?"

"She does not want a cookie," Cybil says.

"I think she does." I go to the display case in the front and take out a plain sugar cookie, then break off a tiny piece and give it to her. Just like that, instant happiness. She reaches for more while dancing from side to side. And Cybil, of course, rolls her eyes. "So what are you guys going to do now?"

"I have to work, so Tanner is going to hang with Claire," Cybil says, leaning into her husband.

"Do you need me to help with anything?" I ask, because each time I've asked if she needs me to do anything, she's said no, which makes me feel kind of useless.

"I should be okay. I just need to get some photos taken for my website and some fabric cut for the next round of bags I plan on making."

"I should be off around four today, so I can help you if you're still working when I get home."

"Thanks, I might take you up on that if you don't mind," she says. Then we look to the door when it opens, and I watch Liam, the owner, walk in with a scowl on his face directed at me.

"I have a bone to pick with you, young lady." He wags his finger at me, and I blink at him. "You didn't tell me that you were going to be quitting."

"That's because I'm not quitting." I pass Claire and her cookie off to Tanner.

"Tony and Katie told me that you are renting the space next door."

"Me and my best friend, Cybil, are going to be renting it." I wave my hand out to where Cybil is standing, and she waves at him. "Cybil, you remember Liam. Liam, Cybil, her husband, Tanner, and my niece, Claire," I introduce, then continue after everyone says hi. "I don't know why Katie or Tony told you that I'm quitting. I'm still going to be working here, or that's my plan anyways."

"They didn't exactly say you were quitting, just that you were starting your own business. I assumed that you would not want to work here."

"You assumed wrong." I plant my hands on my hips. "And I hope you know I wouldn't just up and quit on you without giving you a heads-up. Plus I like working here." And I do—making coffee might not be the most exciting job someone could ever have, but I've enjoyed every day that I've worked, plus Tony and Katie have started to grow on me, even if they do call me old all the damn time. Even after I pointed out that I'm only ten years older than them.

"What kind of store are you opening?" Liam asks, ignoring my rant.

"It will be a kind of catchall with books and gifts and stuff."

"You know what goes great with books?" he asks, then answers before I can. "Coffee."

"Coffee and books do go great together," I agree, and he turns to look at the wall behind where Cybil and Tanner are standing.

"We could take out this wall, and then we could have both."

"What?" I laugh, thinking he's joking.

"You sell books, and I sell coffee; who doesn't like to sit down with a latte and a book? It would be the perfect setup, and we would both get more business."

"You're being serious?" My stomach feels funny as I rest my hand over it.

"I don't joke when it comes to my business."

"Well, I don't know that the owner of the building would be okay with us taking down this wall."

"My family owns this building—actually, most of the buildings on this block. I'm sure I could talk them around." He shrugs, and I look at Cybil, wanting to see what she is thinking about all of this. I mean, Liam is not wrong; people do love coffee and books, which is why there's typically a coffee shop inside every big bookstore there is. And having a coffee shop linked to our store would draw more people inside.

"If we can make it happen, I say let's go for it," Cybil says, and I look at Liam.

"I think I love the idea, but we will have to sit down and go over the exact details of everything and see if it's even possible to join the spaces together."

"I'm going to make a few phone calls," he tells me, then looks at Cybil and Tanner. "It was nice meeting you both." He heads for his office, and I watch him go while shaking my head.

"Well." I turn back and meet Tanner's gaze. "Do you think that wall is load bearing?"

"Even if it is, the cost of putting in a support beam would be worth it." He wraps his arm around Cybil's shoulders.

"I have no clue what he's talking about. I couldn't agree more." Cybil leans into her husband, and I laugh. Then we all look at the door when a customer walks in. "We'll let you get back to work, but call me if Liam says anything."

"I will." I kiss Claire before they go, then get the man who came in his drink, which is just a coffee with cream and sugar. As he hangs out at one of the tables working on his laptop, I restock everything, and then not long afterward, Tony and Katie arrive, bringing with them a crowd of their friends. Thankfully the two of them are quick behind the counter, so it doesn't take long to get everyone served.

With the shop full and Katie and Tony chatting with their class-mates from school, I hang in the back and listen to them, realizing that nothing much has changed since I was a teenager. Who's dating who and where everyone is hanging out for the weekend are still two of the most important topics of conversation. One thing that is different is the constant photo taking and the sending of messages even to people who are sitting right next to you. That is something I will probably never really get on board with.

"Jade." I look toward Liam's office when he calls my name and find him planted in the doorway. "Can you come in here for a minute?"

"Sure." I notice Katie and Tony share a worried look. "It's fine," I assure them, setting down the rag that was in my hand before I head to the office. When I get inside, I close the door behind me and then lean against it.

"I've made a few calls, and we are all set if you're really serious about this."

"Really?" I try to keep my composure when I really want to jump up and down. I know having other girls selling items out of the store will help us to gain more customers and hopefully come out ahead each month budget-wise, but having the coffee shop, which is already established, attached would be huge for us.

"Really. Now, we will have to sit down with a lawyer and work out all the details, but I don't see that being a problem as long as we agree that we will only be joined in space, not in profit or loss."

"I agree with that completely, and I know Cybil will as well," I say quietly, and he gives me a soft smile.

"One more thing."

"Yeah?"

"I'd still want you to work for me. You're the first person I've hired who's been reliable and who's gotten along with my grandkids. I don't want to lose you."

"I love this job," I tell him quietly. "And as long as it doesn't become too much for me to work at both the store and here, I'll stay."

"Good." He stands and gives me a hug. "I have a good feeling about this."

"Me too." I let him go, then step back so that he can open the door. When we get out front, he hugs Katie and gives Tony a pat on the back before saying goodbye and taking off. I look at the clock and notice that it's time for me to take off as well.

"Is everything okay?" Katie asks me quietly, and I feel Tony get close.

"Absolutely, just talking to your grandpa about some business stuff. I'm sure he will tell you about it."

"Cool." Tony nudges my shoulder. "Do you wanna practice the dance I was trying to teach you before you take off?"

"I think I'm good."

"Come on, don't you want to be famous?"

"I have absolutely zero desire to become famous," I assure him as the door dings. My eyes go to it automatically, and my heart starts to pound as I watch Maverick walk in.

"Your guy is here," Katie tells me, like I didn't notice.

Ignoring her, I take off my apron and hang it on one of the hooks, then grab my coat and put it on, saying to Tony, "Don't forget to take out the trash tonight."

"Shit, did I forget last night?"

"You did." I grab my bag. "Are you two good here?"

"Yep."

"Cool, I'll see you both tomorrow." I head around the counter and meet Maverick halfway across the room. As soon as I'm in front of him, he leans in like he is going to kiss me but stops himself.

"Can we talk?" he asks, his eyes scanning my face, and I nod.

"Sure." I lead the way outside and feel his hand against my lower back as we walk down the sidewalk toward where my car is parked.

"I need to apologize about last night."

"Okay." I peek up at him and try to read his expression, which is pretty pointless. He's not a man who is easy to read.

"I was angry."

"I noticed," I say quietly.

"I wasn't angry with you; I was pissed that I have to keep you like a dirty secret when that's not what you deserve." He stops at my car, and

I turn to face him with my chest feeling funny. A lot of men would be more than okay with having a secret relationship with a woman, but I guess I'm learning that he's not like most men.

"I don't want that, either, but I also want a little time to figure out what is happening here." I motion between us. "Before we involve other people." I wrap my arms around my middle and decide to be honest because, again, I do not need one more man to agree with me until he no longer likes what he's agreed to. "I've had really bad luck when it comes to dating, and things with the men I've gone out with tend to end before they really even start." I drag in a deep breath, then let it out, holding his gaze. "I don't want to tell people that you and I are seeing each other, then next week have to tell them that we are not anymore. Not only would that be embarrassing for me, it might be really uncomfortable for everyone else."

"All right." His eyes stay locked on mine, and I frown.

"All right?"

"I get where you're coming from. So for now we will keep things just between us."

"You said that before, but you got angry at me for reminding you that that was the deal we made," I point out softly, and his expression gentles.

"Yeah, but you just explained your reason for us keeping this quiet." He steps toward me. "I'm not saying I like it, but I get it now." His hand comes up to wrap around the side of my neck. "I just want you to know that I'm not going to keep us a secret forever; that's not going to work for me."

My heart pounds as I look into his eyes. I've never had someone look at me the way he is right now. "Why do I suddenly feel like I'm in over my head?"

He grins at that question, then dips his chin and brushes his lips across mine without answering me. When he pulls back, he keeps his face close. "Are you good with me stopping by your place this evening?"

"I'm good with that," I tell him quietly, and he kisses me once more before he steps back, letting his hand slide away.

"I'll send you a message when I'm on my way."

"Okay." I turn to open the door to my car, and then once I'm inside, he shuts it for me, then watches as I back out of my parking spot. I wave as I leave, then head out of the parking lot, hoping like heck that for once my instincts are right and that he's not too good to be true.

∽

After changing into a pair of sweats and a cutoff sweatshirt, I take out my contacts and put on my glasses, then walk out of my bathroom. Maverick sent me a message ten minutes ago letting me know that he was on his way and that he was bringing a movie, so I decided to get comfortable.

I go to the fridge and grab a soda, then put a bag of popcorn in the microwave and start it. As it pops, I clean up my dishes from this morning, then pick up the living room. When I got home from work, Cybil was still in her office, so I hung out there with her, helping her cut fabric while we talked about the conversation I'd had with Liam. Like I'd figured she would do, she agreed that we should move forward but make sure that we have a lawyer draw up the contract between us so that we are all safe.

After that we sat on my couch with my computer and went over the shelving layout for the store and decided on a paint color for the walls, along with a wallpaper design for two accent walls, a very pretty black, gold, and floral design that is timeless in style. Honestly, while she was here, we both lost track of time, and it wasn't until Tanner called to check on her that we both realized it was already seven in the evening. Time for Claire to take her nightly bath, then get to bed after a story and bottle.

Hearing a knock, I toss the stuff in my hands toward my bed, and Pebbles, who is lying curled up on one of my pillows, gives me a dirty look. "Sorry, I didn't mean to interrupt your sleep," I tell him, and his tail wags. I head for the door, and he hops down to follow me, so I pick him up, not wanting him to run out of the house. My old apartment in Oregon had a small, fenced backyard, so even if he did get out, he couldn't go far and never seemed much inclined to go outside anyway. Here it's a different story. I don't know if it's the scent of the wildlife in the forest beyond the front door or what, but he's venturing a little farther every day and staying outside longer as well.

"Hey," I greet, opening the door, and Maverick's gaze roams over my face and hair.

"I didn't know you wore glasses."

"I keep my contacts in most of the time, but my eyes were starting to bug me." I shrug, stepping aside to let him in, and shut the door. "I think it's because I was on the computer for a while and I'm not used to that," I babble, not sure what to make of the look he's giving me.

"I didn't think you could be cuter. I was wrong." He slides his hand around my waist, making contact with skin, and I shiver from his touch and the coldness of his palm against my bare waist. "I like them."

"Thanks," I say quietly as he leans in to touch his lips to mine, then takes Pebbles from me because he's making a fuss.

"What were you working on?" he asks, taking off his jacket and kicking off his boots when we get into my place.

"Cybil was over, and we were going over the layout of the store, the paint colors, and wallpaper stuff." I walk to the microwave and pull out the bag of popcorn, then get a bowl to dump it in. "And you'll never believe what happened today." I glance over my shoulder at him.

"What happened?"

"Liam, my boss, suggested that we open up the wall between the store and the coffee shop, and since his family owns the building, he was able to call them and get approval to do it."

"Really?"

"That's what I said, because that kind of thing just doesn't happen, but he's serious. Now we just have to talk to a lawyer and get everything down in writing. If it does happen, it will be awesome for us, especially with us just starting out. The coffee shop might not be busy all day, but it is steady, and so while people wait for their drink, they can browse the store and hopefully buy something."

"That would be good," he says as I carry my bowl with me to the couch, where he's sitting with Pebbles.

"Do you want something to drink?" I ask, realizing how rude it is I didn't offer before.

"I'll take a soda," he says, so I hand him the popcorn, then go to the fridge and grab one for him, then go back to the couch and take a seat. "Tanner called me this evening and asked me to meet him over at the store tomorrow to help him get the wall down."

I grin. "I don't think I've ever been so excited about construction in my life." I lean into him. "One of these days I really am going to bake you some store-bought cookie dough."

"I'm looking forward to that." He gives me a soft look.

"So what movie did you bring?" I ask before digging into the popcorn.

"You'll see." He moves to the DVD player and then grabs the remote, and after a minute the movie comes on. As we watch a group of kids find out they have unknowingly gotten superpowers from the crash site of a UFO, I eat my popcorn, then put the bowl aside. I get up and turn out the lights, then grab my blanket from my bed, and when I get back to the couch, he pulls me down to lie with him, tucked against his side, down the length of his body.

As the movie plays, my eyes drift closed. All I can think is that this thing between him and me is comfortable; I don't feel stressed or anxious when I'm with him. I'm not worried that I'm not dressed right or that I didn't put in enough effort. It feels good. Spending time with him feels good. I just hope it continues to feel that way.

Chapter 13

MAVERICK

I take one last swing at the wall, then hand Tanner the sledgehammer and wipe my face on the underside of my shirt to get rid of the dust and sweat.

"I thought I saw your truck drive by the house last night," Tanner says, taking a swing at the wall, which is only partially down.

"You did." I don't lie—first, he would know if I did; second, he's like a brother to me and one of the few people I've ever trusted in my life. I would never do anything to jeopardize that trust. Not with him and not with Blake.

"You're spending time with Jade." He stops to look at me, and I lift my chin in an affirmative. "You wanna talk about it?"

"Nope," I say, and he smiles.

"Right, just be careful."

"Why are we being careful?" Blake walks in with Mason right behind him, and they both drop the stuff they brought along with them on the pile of shit Tanner and I brought.

"Mav is spending time with Jade."

"Cybil's best friend?" Blake asks, looking at me, and I shake my head. Maybe Jade was right about men gossiping more than women do.

"Yep," Tanner says.

"She seemed sweet the couple times I met her." Blake walks over and takes the sledgehammer from Tanner.

"She is. She's also been through a lot; Cybil and her parents have been worried about her."

"What happened?" Blake asks.

"She lost her bookstore back in Oregon around the same time her ex screwed her over."

"Her ex screwed her over?" I ask, and Tanner's gaze comes to me.

"Yeah, he borrowed some money to start up a business and didn't pay it back even after she explained that she needed it to hold her over until she found another job," Tanner says, and fuck if it doesn't feel like a kick to the gut to learn that from him. It also makes more sense why she said she didn't have a great track record with men and why she wasn't big on the idea of dating me.

"You guys can't let anyone know that her and I are seeing each other. She wants to keep it quiet for now."

"I think Margret knows that something is going on between you two," Mason says, and I look at him. "She said she saw you two kiss."

"Well, tell her to keep quiet about it for now."

"Will do." He shrugs.

"Cybil also knows something is up. She noticed you going down to her place a couple of times," Tanner says, and I cross my arms over my chest.

"Right, then everyone, just do me a favor and pretend like you don't know something is happening between us."

"You got it," Tanner mutters, sharing a smile with Blake and Mason.

"How are the wedding plans going?" Tanner asks Blake, and he pulls the sledgehammer out of the wall, taking a huge chunk of board with it.

"I guess it's going all right. Mom and Everly both stopped asking for my opinion around the time that the color scheme was being picked out." He hands the hammer to Mason, then steps back. "I told Everly we should have just gone to Vegas, but she wasn't having it."

"It will be worth it in the end," Tanner tells him while grabbing a large black garbage bag.

"I just want to marry her and adopt Sam; I don't need the show."

"Happy wife, happy life, man," Mason says, and Blake looks at him.

"Yeah, are you going to stop playing house with my sister and put a ring on her finger?" he asks, and I wait, actually really interested in his answer. Blake and Mason were friends growing up, and with Margret being Blake's twin sister, she was always around as well, only she was off limits. That doesn't mean that we all didn't see that Margret and Mason should be together. But Margret had just ended a seriously fucked-up relationship with the father of her daughter, and Blake had made it clear he didn't want his friends dating his little sister. So needless to say, it took a while for the two of them to admit how they felt about each other.

"I plan on talking to your dad soon," Mason tells him, and I rub the center of my chest. Blake and Margret's dad has been diagnosed with cancer, something he kept a secret from everyone, but like all secrets it eventually came out. So far he's been doing okay with the new treatment they are using, but I think we're all worried that that could change at any time. "I was thinking of asking her on Christmas."

"Well, okay then," Blake says, then adds: "You have my blessing."

"I'm past the point of caring if I have your blessing or not," Mason tells him, and we all chuckle.

"Do you guys realize that we are all dropping like flies?" Tanner looks around the group, and then his eyes land on me. "Looks like you're gonna be up next, brother."

"I'm never getting married," I tell him, and he raises a brow. "Don't get me wrong, I'm happy for you guys and glad that you've found what you have, but I don't see that in the cards for me," I say, ignoring that voice in the back of my head, the one reminding me that I also never chased a woman before, but look at me now. Basically stalking a woman just to be in her presence for a few minutes, then acting like an ass when she reminds me that I agreed to keep things between us, all because I want everyone to know that she's mine.

"We'll see," Blake mutters.

"How about we focus on getting this shit done." I take the trash bag from Tanner, and the two of us begin to clean up some of the debris from the floor, then put on gloves and start to rip out the wall on the opposite side. By the time we're done clearing out the beams from the center and patching the holes where the wall was attached and along the ceiling, it's getting dark out, and my stomach is rumbling.

"Oh my God," I hear Cybil say and turn to find her, along with Jade, who's holding Claire; Everly, who's got Sam; and Margret with her daughter, Taylor, standing near the front door. "It looks so much bigger." Cybil rushes to Tanner and hugs him while Margret walks to Mason, getting a kiss from him, and Everly goes to Blake.

I watch Jade and the way she watches her friends, and my fingers twitch with the urge to reach for her. Fuck, I'm so fucked—there is no way I will be able to do this for long. We are just a few hours in, and I already want to say *fuck it*, grab her around the waist, and kiss her in front of everyone.

"You guys got a lot done," Jade says, walking Claire over to me when she babbles and holds out her hands in my direction.

"I got God knows what on me, baby, so you're gonna have to keep hold of her," I tell her quietly, and she licks her lips as her eyes drop to my mouth. Good to know I'm not the only one fighting against instinct.

"I'm sure you guys are starving. Do you want to head up to our place? We can stop and get a few pizzas on the way," Cybil suggests to the group.

"That sounds good to me," Blake says, and Mason agrees.

"Awesome," Cybil says, then looks around. "Do you want us to help you clean up any of this stuff?"

"We're going to leave it for now. Tomorrow I'll pick up the paint while Mav and Blake patch up the holes in the walls; then we'll lay down a couple coats."

"That fast?" Jade asks.

"Paint is easy; building all the shelves you want is going to take time," Tanner tells her, then comes over to kiss Claire on the cheek when she starts to babble "Dada" over and over again.

"Well, okay, I think us girls should go pick up food while you guys do whatever you're doing. Then we'll meet you up at the house," Cybil says, and the girls all agree before saying their goodbyes and taking off.

"I feel like we need to make a bet," Blake says as we're heading out of the building a while later, and we all look at him. "I bet Mav cracks in a week and this whole keep-him-and-Jade-a-secret thing goes out the window."

"Damn, you're generous. I say it happens tonight," Mason says, then looks at me. "No offense, man, but I could tell that you were working at keeping yourself in check when she came in."

"I give it until Jade gives him the go-ahead, unless something happens and he's forced to break cover," Tanner says.

"Glad to know at least one person has faith in me," I mutter, breaking off from the group when I reach my truck. Then I call out that I'll see them at Tanner's as they head to their vehicles.

~

I park in front of Jade's place and get out of my truck, then head up to the door. She sent me a text while we were sitting around with everyone eating pizza and hanging out, asking if I wanted to come to her place to watch a movie. She didn't even have to ask. Spending time with her without being able to touch her was a special kind of torture, so there was no way I was going home tonight without being able to get my hands on her.

I get to the door and knock, then wait for her to answer. It takes a minute to hear the door to her place open, and a second later she's there. My gut tightens like it did last night at seeing her in her glasses with her hair in a messy bun and her face makeup-free. Fuck, she's beautiful.

"Hey." She smiles, and without thinking, I place my hand against her belly, walking her back into the house, then kick the door closed behind me before I take her mouth in a deep kiss. Like she's done every time I've kissed her, her body melts against mine, and she holds on tight. Moving my hands from her waist to her ass, I slide them down to the back of her thighs and pick her up off the ground. Without losing her mouth, I walk her into her apartment and head for the bed. As soon as the backs of my knees meet the mattress, I fall back with her on top of me, the sound she makes causing my cock, which is already hard, to harden further.

"I wanted to kiss you so bad earlier," she tells me as my mouth trails down her throat to the tops of her breast and her nails dig into my chest.

"I wouldn't have stopped you." I pull back to look at her as her thighs tighten on the outsides of mine. After slipping off her glasses, I place them on the side table, then pull the hair tie out of her hair so that it hangs like a curtain around us. "So fucking pretty."

I hold on to her hips, then roll her to her back. My mouth travels from hers down her neck, nipping and licking until I reach the top of the tank she put on when she got home. Grasping her breast, I listen to her moan, then pull the material of her shirt down, exposing her and watching her nipple tighten before I cover it with my mouth. She whimpers as her eyes squeeze closed, and she presses her head back into the pillow. Moving to her other breast, I lick and suck her nipple, feeling it harden against my tongue while she lifts her legs and circles my waist.

I move to my knees, then slide her shorts and panties down her legs and toss them to the floor before I strip my shirt off over my head.

Coming back down on top of her, I kiss her deep, then move my mouth down her neck to her breast, once more licking, sucking her nipples while her fingers slide through my hair.

"Maverick," she pants, lifting her hips, trying to get closer, while my cock tests the limits of my zipper.

"Fuck," I bite out. I wasn't planning on this, but I'm too far gone in her. "Gotta get my jeans off and a condom." My mouth finds hers, and I kiss her deep, then pull away and get off the bed, grabbing a condom out of my wallet and tossing it to the bed while I watch *her* watch *me* shuck off my jeans. "Shirt off, baby," I order, and she sits up, slipping her shirt off over her head. As soon as I've got my jeans off, I get back between her legs and place my mouth against hers while using my weight to force her back. Her legs wrap around my hips, and my cock bumps her entrance. Fuck, she's wet and warm, and I want nothing more than to sink into her.

"Jesus, I swear you're trying to kill me." I bite her earlobe. "I can't decide if I should eat you or fuck you first."

"Fuck me." She tightens her hold on me, and I move my hand between us, running my fingers through her folds, then circling her clit.

"Are you sure you don't want my mouth right here?" I roll her clit, and her neck arches. "You don't want me to eat you first?" I slide two fingers inside of her, and her core tightens as she shakes her head back and forth. "You're right—your pussy is hungry, baby."

I play with her for a minute, watching until she's right on the edge before I reach for the condom and rip it open with my teeth. When I have it on, I hold the tip at her entrance and enter her slowly, when all I want to do is ram home. Her fingers dig into my shoulder, and her hips lift off the bed, sending me even deeper, testing my control.

Needing to take my mind off the urge to come already, I kiss her deep, rolling my tongue across hers, and she raises her head to kiss me back, then gasps as I sink into her completely.

She fits me perfectly, feels as perfect under me as she did lying against me last night, when we were doing nothing more than watching a movie. When I pull back, her lashes flutter open, and her eyes meet mine, causing an odd sensation to fill my chest.

"Oh God," she moans, scratching her nails down my back while I slide out, then back in, then grab her hands and pull both of them up over her head.

"Keep your hands here. If you keep touching me, I won't be able to keep it together, and things will be over before they start," I tell her, and she grabs hold of her pillow. I swivel my hips and watch her expression, finding out what she likes and doesn't, then move my mouth to her breast and pull it between my lips. As she moans and whimpers, I move faster and faster, feeling her pussy getting hotter and tighter. When I know she's on the edge, I slide my hand between us and lean back to watch as I roll her clit and bottom out deep inside her over and over again.

She's perfect. Everything about her is perfect.

My spine starts to tingle while her legs tighten around mine, and I know that she is just as close as I am.

"Mav."

"I got you. Let go." I kiss her while her walls tighten so much that it's almost painful to move. "Fuck, baby," I groan, watching her face and feeling her core convulse as she starts to come.

Picking up speed, I grab her behind her knee and drop my mouth down to hers, thrusting twice more before I plant myself deep inside, her orgasm milking mine from me. With my chest heaving, I use what little strength I have left to roll to my back and bring her with me, her core still pulsing around my length as she falls against me. With both of us breathing heavy, I feel her shiver, so I reach for the blanket tossed on the end of the bed and drag it over us.

"Am I too heavy?" she asks, sounding sleepy, and I smile.

"Hell no." I kiss the top of her head and feel her cheek move.

"You know, I didn't think you were even a little interested in me."

"What?" I laugh because I'm still semihard inside her.

"You chucked me on my chin like I was a kid sister. I didn't think you were even attracted to me."

"I'm definitely attracted to you."

"I know that now, but I couldn't tell before. You're very hard to read."

"I think I told you I was trying to keep my distance."

"Why?"

Because you're the kind of woman I could lose myself in. "Like you, I didn't want to complicate things."

"Now you do?"

"Yeah, now I do," I tell her softly, then roll her to her back and kiss her quickly. "I'll be right back. I need to take care of the condom." I kiss her forehead, then knife off the bed.

"I'll be here," she mumbles, and I grin as I head for the bathroom. After taking care of the condom, I grab a rag from the shelf and toss it in the sink, turning on the hot water. I carry it back to the bed and grasp her ankle, making her jump.

"Just cleaning you up," I tell her, and she gives me a soft look filled with surprise. After wiping her gently, I take the rag back to the bathroom and toss it into the sink, then head across the room to flip off the lights before I get back in bed with her and pull her against me.

"By the way, thank you for helping Tanner with all the stuff at the store today."

"You're welcome, baby." I kiss her forehead and smooth my fingers up and down her arm.

Lying there, I listen to her breath even out and feel her body relax completely against me. I should get up, get dressed, and go, but instead of doing what I should do, I close my eyes and fall asleep with her in my arms, and I sleep better than I ever have before.

Chapter 14

JADE

With my cheek pressed to Maverick's bare chest, I shiver as his fingers dance over my hip, then laugh when my stomach grumbles.

"Hungry?" he asks quietly, sounding like he's half-asleep, and I tip my head back to look at him.

"You've had me trapped in your bed since I arrived here this morning under the pretense that you were making me breakfast, and it's now noon."

"Poor baby." He grins, pulling me up his body to bring my face closer to his, and I run my fingers through the hair at the side of his head. "What time are you meeting Cybil?"

"Two." I move to straddle his waist and get lost in the look in his eyes. God, but I really love the way he looks at me.

"Then I need to get you fed." He rolls me to my back, making me squeak in surprise. "Even though I really just want to keep you trapped here under me." I raise my hips, letting him know that I wouldn't exactly be opposed to that, but as he leans down to kiss me, my stomach grumbles again. "Let's get you something to eat." He kisses me quickly, then pulls me up out of bed with him. Once we are both standing, he hands me the T-shirt he had on when I arrived and puts on a pair of his boxers before grabbing my hand to lead me out of the room.

When we get into the kitchen, he urges me to sit on one of the chairs at the counter by crowding me back into it and kissing me once more. "Are you okay with grilled cheese?" he leans back to ask while keeping his body pressed against mine.

"Yes."

"Good." He lets me go, then walks over to the stove, places a pan down, and turns on the heat. I get up to get a glass of water, then sit and take a sip to hide my smile as I watch him butter four slices of bread. The first time I was here and he cooked for me, much like he is right now, shirtless with his feet bare, comfortable in his environment, I remember being so sure that he wasn't interested in me. Now I've kissed and touched every inch of him more than once, and every time we are together, it's better than the last, and that's saying something, since each time I've been with him, it's been spectacular.

"What's with the smile?" he asks, meeting my gaze as he goes to the fridge to grab some cheese, and I shrug one shoulder.

"Nothing, just happy," I admit, and his face gets soft before he turns to tuck the cheese in the middle of the bread and then places both sandwiches on the pan.

"Me too." His voice is quiet, and then we both look at his phone on the counter next to me when it starts to ring. "You wanna tell me who that is?" He turns back to the stove, and I flip his phone over, and my heart feels funny when I see the name Lizzy on the screen.

"Umm, it's someone named Lizzy. She's FaceTiming you."

"My sister." He walks over to me with a smile and grabs the phone off the counter before sliding his finger across the screen. As soon as the call connects, what sounds like chaos fills the room.

"Hey, baby brother," a woman shouts over the noise in the background behind her. "You haven't called me to check in for a couple of days."

"Sorry about that," Maverick tells her, moving back to the stove, and with his back to me as he looks into the phone, I can see his sister on the screen. Even from where I'm sitting, I can see that she has the same dark hair and striking features as her brother. "I've been helping Tanner with a project."

"Mom, is that Uncle Maverick?" a little boy shouts.

Then another yells, "I want to talk to him."

"You'll have to wait a minute. I'm talking to him right now," Lizzy says as two little faces fight to get in front of the screen.

"Who's the girl at your house?" one of the boys yells.

"Wait, there is a girl at your house?" Lizzy shouts, and my eyes widen as her face appears in front of the boys on the screen. As Maverick turns to me, I wonder if I should duck under the counter but don't get the chance when he walks over to where I am with his phone in hand.

"Lizzy, I'd like you to meet Jade. Babe, this is my sister, Lizzy." He places the phone in front of my face, and I'm sure I look like a deer trapped in headlights.

"Umm." I clear my throat. "Nice to meet you."

"You too," she says, looking at me, and then her attention goes to Maverick. "You have a woman at the house?"

"I do." He turns the screen so that it's angled toward the wall, then kisses me swiftly on the lips before he goes back to the stove. "I'm gonna call you back, Lizzy. Jade and I were just getting ready to eat."

"You better call me," she says sternly.

"I'll call," he assures her, then adds: "Kiss the boys and tell them we'll talk later."

"I will," she agrees before the screen goes black.

"You do know that I'm wearing nothing but your shirt, have sex hair, and my makeup is probably a mess, and you just introduced me to your sister." I lift my hair up and go to tie it into a bun but stop when I realize my rubber band isn't on my wrist. "And you know if you keep taking my hair ties and tossing them every time we're together, I'm not going to have any left."

"Or you could stop wearing your hair up when we're together." He puts both grilled-cheese sandwiches on one plate. "And your makeup is just fine, you don't have sex hair, and my sister doesn't know that you've only got on my tee. She only saw your face."

"But I know all those things," I point out as he rips off a couple of paper towels, then grabs a soda from the fridge.

"Come on." He motions with his chin for me to follow him, ignoring my comment.

"Where are we going?"

"Back to bed," he says, so I pick up my water glass and walk behind him to his room. As I get on the bed and sit next to him cross-legged, Lizzy's comment comes back to me.

"You don't bring women to your house?"

"Nope." He picks up one of the sandwiches and wraps half of it in a paper towel before passing me the plate and other sandwich.

"Never?" This is shocking to me; he's a good-looking man, and even without a whole bunch of words, I have no doubt he'd have no trouble sealing the deal with any woman anywhere.

"Never."

"Why not?"

"I don't like women in my space," he says, and I blink. Since we decided to see where this goes, I've been to his place more than once, and on what I consider our first date, he said he wanted me to spend the night the next Saturday. He never acted like he didn't want me around or like me being here made him uncomfortable.

"You're the exception, baby. I like having you here with me," he says like he's read my mind.

"You like having me here with you?" I repeat while my chest warms, that feeling blocking out the urge to ask why he doesn't like women in his space.

"I do." He nudges the plate on my lap. "Now eat before your sandwich gets cold."

Figuring that is his way of saying he's done with the conversation, I pick up my sandwich and take a bite. Like everything else he's made for me, it's delicious.

"You know you're gonna give me an ego."

"What?" I laugh as I swallow my bite.

"You moan every time I cook for you, like you haven't eaten in days and it's the best thing you've ever had in your life."

"You're a good cook."

"It's grilled cheese. You made us grilled cheese a couple nights ago at your place." I did do that; it was after us doing exactly what we did today, and I was starving, so I made us something simple that I knew I couldn't mess up.

"I guess, but yours just taste better." I take another bite, and then once I swallow, I ask softly, "Are you okay with your sister knowing about me?"

"I'm the one who introduced you two, babe. I'm good with it. I think the real question is—are you okay with it?"

"Yes." Surprisingly it's the truth. I might not be ready to tell my best friend about him and me, but I don't mind his sister knowing about us. Really, him being so willing to tell the woman who raised him about us makes me feel more secure.

"When she and her husband bring the boys up for New Year's, I'd like you to meet them."

"I'd like that," I say, hoping like heck that when the New Year rolls around in a few months, he and I will still be together, because the thought that we won't makes me feel nauseous.

"Come here," he orders, wrapping his hand around the side of my neck, and I lean toward him. As soon as I'm close, he kisses me, soft and sweet, then holds my forehead against his. "We're good."

"We are," I agree with a small smile, and he gives my neck a squeeze, then one more touch of his lips, before he lets me go so we can both finish eating. When we're done, we laze in bed for a while longer, and then I get up and get dressed so I can make it in time to meet Cybil at the shop, even though I want nothing more than to stay with him in bed the rest of the day. The only thing that makes leaving a little easier is him letting me know that he'll be at my place this evening.

~

"I thought you said that this was supposed to be easy." I glare down at Cybil from where I'm standing on the top of a ladder, holding a long piece of paper that is heavier than it looks. Either that or my arms are weaker than they should be and I really need to start thinking about working out.

"I didn't say it was going to be easy—the website we ordered it from did." She glares back at me before going back to using a roller brush to remove the bumps and bubbles from the wallpaper we chose for our accent walls. "Maybe we are doing something wrong."

"Or maybe we should have asked the guys to do this," I mumble, looking behind me to the shelves that now line the walls. Shelves the guys installed around the store in just a few days. I mean, they still need to be painted, but the work they did in such a short amount of time is seriously impressive.

And then there are Cybil and me. The two of us have been here for almost three hours, and we haven't even finished covering one wall.

"Neither of us has ever hung wallpaper before."

"I know." I look down at her as she uses a sharp blade to cut off the excess paper at the bottom near the baseboard. "But I feel like this is much more difficult than it should be." I start down the ladder, slowly using the large sponge we bought to go over the paper one last time. When I reach the floor, we both step back to examine our work. "I guess it doesn't look bad." I tip my head one way, then the other, like it will help me know if it's crooked or not.

"I think it looks great." She wraps her arm around my waist, then rests her head on my shoulder. "I don't know about you, but I'm tired."

"I imagine you are. I'm exhausted, and I don't have a baby who keeps me up half the night." I rest my head on top of hers. "Do you want to keep going, or do you want to call it a day and get back to this tomorrow?"

"I say we finish this wall." She lets me go. "We are so close; I think we could be done in an hour." She starts to unroll some more of the paper, so I stir the glue and start to paint it in even strokes across the white back like the directions suggested. Once I have an even coat, I go back up the ladder, because apparently my best friend is now afraid of heights. After I reach the top, she hands me the top edge of the paper, and we both work to get it lined up with the edge of the last sheet we hung. Just as we start to get it in place, a cool gust of wind floats into the room, and I turn to find Everly and Margret coming inside. I smile at the two of them.

"Please tell me that you guys came to help," I say in lieu of a greeting.

"We didn't, but we can," Margret says, taking off her coat, and Everly does the same, the two of them dropping them where Cybil and I left ours on the floor. Then they come to where we are.

"We actually came to talk to you guys about my bachelorette party," Everly says, looking up at me, then asks, "How can I help?"

"Can you grab the roller and hand it to me?" I ask, and she looks around until she finds it, then brings it over and places it in my open hand.

"Are you having a party?" Cybil asks Everly when I finish rolling out the top and hand the roller down to her.

"She is," Margret answers for her. "She wanted us to just get our nails done and have a late lunch, but I told her that's unacceptable. She needs a proper party, so I've decided to take over the planning myself."

"Should we be worried?" Cybil asks, and Margret rolls her eyes.

"I've already promised my brother that I wouldn't do anything that could lead to any one of us spending the night in jail, so you have nothing to worry about."

"Is ending up in jail something that happens regularly when people go out with you?" I ask Margret, and she looks up at me and smiles wide.

"No, that's normally something I do when I'm on my own," she says, and I smile back, then grab the sponge when Cybil hands it to me. Darn, with Margret and Everly here, we are already doing better than we were.

When I'm done smoothing out the top, I get down off the ladder and roll out the next piece of paper and start to paint it with the sticky glue as Cybil trims the bottom edge.

"Well, you know I'll be there," Cybil says, then looks at me, and I shift back to rest my bottom on my heels.

"I'll be there if you want me to be."

"Of course I want you to be there," Everly says, helping me lift the paper up off the ground. The truth is, I'm still trying to get used to how quickly everyone has accepted me. I know that it's because of Cybil, but I appreciate how they have all welcomed me in as a part of the group.

"It's going to be awesome," Margret says as I head up the ladder once more. "I'm going to plan a whole day of pampering, then a night out on the town that I'm sure we will all remember."

"A night to remember without any of us ending up in jail," Everly clarifies.

"Will you stop saying that like I'm going to get us all arrested," Margret grouches. "I mean, jeez. A girl ends up in the back of a police cruiser one time, and all the sudden she can't be trusted."

"Okay, so when are we doing this?" Cybil asks.

"The Saturday after next, since the following weekend we will all be headed to the lake house for the wedding," Margret tells her, and I make a mental note so that I can make sure I'm not working on Sunday in case I'm hungover. Not that I really work weekends, since Tony and Katie tend to take those days.

"You're going to come to the wedding, right, Jade?" Everly asks, and I look down at her.

"I didn't plan on it," I say. Then I add, "Not that I don't want to be there. I just don't want to intrude."

"You're not intruding. We would love for you to come."

"Are you sure?"

"Absolutely." She smiles as I grab the roller from Cybil. "You could bring a date if you'd like."

My stomach bottoms out at that offer, and I glance quickly to Cybil. I still haven't admitted to her that Maverick and I have been seeing each other, and the more time goes by, the more I feel like a horrible friend. For once in my life, I feel like I have it all. But the truth is I keep waiting for the other shoe to drop. I keep waiting for something to happen that will knock me off my high horse of happiness. And I'm honestly afraid that the thing that I'm going to lose is Maverick; even with him making plans for future dates, I worry that he's going to realize what a mess I am and decide that he and I don't work.

"Thanks for the offer, but if I can get the time off, it will just be me," I tell her, and I swear I catch Margret and Cybil sharing a look, but I ignore it as I get down off the ladder. There is no way they could know. Right?

"That paper is beautiful," Margret says as we all stand back to examine the now-finished wall.

"It is, isn't it?" Cybil says, and I couldn't agree more. The black background with colorful flowers and gold swirls totally pops, especially with the light gray, almost white, that the rest of the walls are painted.

"So what's next?" Everly asks.

"Well, we were going to quit after this wall was done, but if you guys don't mind helping us, we could knock out the other wall."

"I can stay. Just let me call Blake and let him know that I won't be home until a little later," Everly says.

"I'll call Mason and do the same," Margret tells us, and both girls go to where their things are across the room while Cybil and I take the ladder and stuff to the other wall we want to cover.

Then, with the girls' help, we knock out the rest of the work within just a couple of hours, and as we lock up the store when we're finished, all I can think is maybe, just maybe, in moving here I will actually have everything I ever wanted and more.

Chapter 15

JADE

I take my cell phone with me along with my cup of coffee to the bathroom, setting the cup on the counter so I can dial my mom's number. When the phone starts to ring, I put the call on speaker and set it down so I can pick up my face cream.

"Hey, honey," Mom answers as I pump some face cream onto my fingers and start to massage it into my skin.

"Hey, are you and Dad all packed?" I ask, picking up my concealer and starting to dot it on my face.

Tomorrow my parents are coming, bringing with them a truckload of the stuff from my old store and killing two birds with one stone while they're here, since they'll be able to hang out with Claire while Cybil and I go out with Everly for her bachelorette party and Tanner goes out with Blake for his bachelor get-together the same night.

"We are, or I am. I've refused to pack for your dad this trip," she grumbles, and I laugh.

"What happened?"

"I asked him what he wanted to put in our suitcase, and he told me to decide. Then I told him that he should tell me since I don't know what he will want to wear every day." She lets out a breath. "After that I told him that I'm not his mother and put all my stuff in a smaller bag."

"Mom, you do realize that you've created that monster? You've always packed for Dad," I remind her.

"Yes, well, now he can pack for himself," she huffs.

"All right," I agree, because my mom is stubborn, and if she has it in her head that she is not going to pack for him, no one will be able to change her mind.

"If it makes you feel better, I've reminded him no less than a dozen times that we are leaving tomorrow so he needs to get his stuff together."

"He's a big boy; he'll figure it out, and if he doesn't, he can go shopping when you guys get here."

"Your dad shop." She laughs, and I smile at my reflection while I lean toward the mirror and apply mascara to my lashes.

"Okay, besides the packing business, are you all ready?"

"Yes, your boxes and things are all in the back of the truck under a tarp, and we've got a kid from town coming over to house-sit for us while we are away, so the dogs will be okay."

"Awesome. I can't wait to see you both."

"We can't wait to see you either."

"You mean you can't wait to see Claire," I say as I grab my blush and start to apply it to the apples of my cheeks.

"She's gotten so big," she says, sounding so happy. "We miss all of our girls."

"We all miss you guys too," I assure her.

"So what are your plans for the day?"

"I'm getting ready to go pick up Cybil. She and I have a meeting with my boss, Liam, to go over the contract he had written up for the coffee shop and the store."

"That's exciting."

"So exciting. I still can't believe how things have just been falling into place."

"You were meant to be there, honey."

"It feels that way," I agree, then look at my reflection and take my hair out of the ponytail I've had it in since last night. Thankfully it doesn't look bad, so I just use a few sprays of dry shampoo and run a brush through it.

"Well, I'll let you go. I need to clean up the house a little before the girl who's house-sitting for us gets here to go over everything she'll need to do while we're away."

"All right, text me tomorrow when you guys leave. I'll be at work, but I'll have my cell phone on me."

"Okay, honey," she agrees, then says quietly, "I love you."

"Love you, too, and I will see you soon. Tell Dad I love him."

"I will."

"And Mom," I call before she can hang up.

"Yeah?"

"Pack for Dad. He loves you."

"Yeah, yeah," she says before she hangs up, and I laugh as I pick up my cup of coffee, then take a sip of it as I head to my room to finish getting ready.

An hour later, sitting on the couch in Liam's living room next to Cybil, I look around the room. On every surface there are photos of Liam and his wife, children, grandkids, and siblings. Along with a few framed black and whites on the wall of the town I now call home before it was even half of what it is now. It's humbling to see so much history in one space, and I'm honestly amazed that Liam is open to change when so many people fight tooth and nail to keep things the way they have always been. The thing about that is nothing ever stays the same.

"Sorry about the wait," Liam says, coming into the room with a tall, good-looking man walking in right behind him. "This is my grandson Jason; he wrote up the contract for us," he says, and Jason looks between Cybil and me.

"It's nice to meet you both."

"You too." I introduce myself and shake his hand, and then Cybil does the same.

"My grandfather explained the situation to me, so I wrote up a pretty simple contract for the three of you to sign." He pulls out a stack of papers and sets them on the coffee table between the couches we are all seated on.

"If this is a simple contract, I'd hate to see a complicated one," I say, and his eyes meet mine.

"Don't be intimidated. I made extra copies so that you could each have a set."

"Cool," I mutter, feeling like a dork, and he grins.

"Like I said, this is pretty simple, but I'm going to go over the most important points." He hands each of us a copy and starts to go over each page one by one. Even as simple as it is, it takes a while for him to get through each page, so an hour has passed by the time he's handing us pens so that we can sign the documents. As I write my name where my name is printed in black ink, butterflies fill my stomach. I still can't believe this is happening.

"Well, that's it." He takes the papers we signed from us and places them back in his folder. "Congratulations, I think that your store and the coffee shop coming together is going to add something extra special to the town."

"We think so too," Cybil tells him, finding my hand where it's resting on the couch between us. I squeeze her fingers, then stand when Liam and Jason do.

"Now we need to figure out when we can rip down that wall between the store and the coffee shop," Liam tells us, but his eyes are on Cybil.

"I'll talk to my husband and see when he thinks he can start." She accepts a kiss to her cheek from Liam when we stop near the front door, and I accept a hug. "I know that he should have some time this week with our parents coming into town." She looks at me. "But I'm not sure how much notice you'll need, since you might have to close the coffee shop for a couple of days while most of the work is done."

"I'll work around his schedule. Just have Jade let me know what days he needs me to close the shop," he tells us, then opens the door, and we step outside.

"We'll let you know," I tell him, and we both wave goodbye before heading down the step to my car. When we get inside, I look over at my best friend and feel tears fill my eyes.

"Do not start crying."

"I'm not going to start crying," I lie, and she shakes her head while her eyes start to water.

"This is going to be amazing."

"It is," I whisper over the lump in my throat.

"I love you." She leans over and wraps her arms around me, and I hug her back. I honestly do not know what I would do without her, but I'm seriously thankful that I will never have to find out. "Now let's go back to the house. I need to talk to my husband and probably figure out some kind of payment plan for all the work he's been doing."

I laugh and let her go, then wipe under my eyes as I start the engine of my car. "You know that man of yours would jump off a cliff if you asked him to."

"I know," she says softly, and I glance over at her. "But I never want him to think I'd expect him to do that."

Shaking my head, I wonder what world she is living in. "For Tanner you raise the sun and set the moon in the sky each night. There is nothing you could ask him to do that would be too much, and I know it's the same for you."

"That's love, right?" she asks quietly. "Putting someone else's wants and needs above your own and hoping they love you enough to do the same in return?"

"I've never experienced that kind of love outside of Mom and Dad before, but I think that's how it's supposed to be," I tell her, wondering what it must feel like to love and be loved so completely.

~

With a plastic container in my hand, I head up the steps at Maverick's house, ignoring the anxiousness in the pit of my stomach. I know that emotion has nothing to do with Maverick but is left over from a previous relationship. One where I showed up at a guy's house hoping to surprise him, only to find that he had another woman over. Which was a shock to me since we were supposed to be exclusive. He just didn't tell me that only I was supposed to be exclusive with him, while he could date anyone he wanted.

After knocking on the door, I stand back and wait, hoping he's home and not out on his property somewhere. I didn't tell him I was coming, since I didn't plan on seeing him until later this evening, when he told me he'd come to my place. Then I went to the grocery store after I dropped Cybil off at the house and passed the premade cookie dough and decided to grab a pack. Honestly I don't even know that he eats cookies; I've never seen the man consume sugar, so I might be eating a dozen chocolate chip cookies on my own. Not that I will be upset about it.

"Hey, baby." He opens the door with a smile that states clearly he's happy to see me. "I was just getting ready to head up the mountain to check the markers the surveyor placed today." He greets me with a kiss, then looks down at my hands. "What's this?"

"Just something I made you." I pass the container over to him as I step into the house, then watch him open the lid.

"You made me cookies?" His eyes meet mine, and the look he gives me makes my cheeks warm. It's stupid, I know. I mean, the guy has seen every single inch of me, and I've never once blushed, but seeing his reaction to me giving him cookies does?

"I baked them; I didn't make them, really," I say as he takes one out and takes a bite. Biting my lip, I watch him chew, then shift on my feet as he swallows.

"Best thing I've tasted in my life besides you," he tells me, his voice deep, and then he wraps his free hand around my waist and tugs me into him so that he can cover my mouth with his. He tastes like him and chocolate, which might be my new favorite thing. "You wanna go for a ride with me?" he asks when he pulls back, and I nod my head.

"Give me five; I just need to grab a different shirt." He kisses me swiftly once more, then turns, heads for the kitchen, and drops the container there. "Be right back."

"I'll be here," I say, and he leaves me at the island before he heads for his room, and I take my purse off my shoulder, setting it on top of the bar. Noticing the blueprints for his new house sitting out and opened on the counter, I smile as I look them over; then my heart does an odd little thump. Where the bathroom for the master is located, a tub has been drawn into the image with black Sharpie. Holy shit.

"Ready?"

I jump at that question and turn to face him.

"Yep." I run my suddenly sweaty hands down the front of my jeans.

"You'll have to stay on the four-wheeler when we get up there," he tells me, looking down at my feet, and I glance down at my bootees, which are not really acceptable for walking anywhere but on the concrete where I wore them today or from my car to his front door.

"That's okay. I don't mind."

"All right," he says as he opens the container of cookies, takes out another, and shoves the whole thing into his mouth. As he chews, he takes my hand and leads me to the front door; then he tells me to wait while he gets the four-wheeler out of the shed. As I stand on his front porch and wait for him, all I can do is think about the bathtub that will now be in his house, a place he's building for the people he cares about.

Chapter 16

JADE

I'm standing with Cybil, Everly, and Margret. The four of us watch my dad, Tanner, Blake, Maverick, and Mason place a large beam in the ceiling between the coffee shop and the store.

I want to cheer them on as they work, but I don't think that would be appropriate, even if I am excited that this is finally getting done. If the wall hadn't been load bearing, the guys probably would have had it out and the space repaired within a couple of days, but the wall was one that provided support, so it took a little longer to get all the stuff to complete the job properly.

As Tanner hammers the beam into place, my eyes go to Maverick, and I watch his muscles flex as he holds his arms over his head. Even with my parents here he's made a point to come spend the evenings with me, and I haven't fallen asleep without him since the first time we slept together.

The only thing that sucks is he's normally gone in the morning before I even wake up. I know I should be relieved that he's not there so questions won't be asked, but I'm not. Even if I'm also not 100 percent sure that I'm ready to tell people that he and I are seeing each other, I've gotten to the point where I no longer care. Things between him and me are good, better than good, really, and even if things tend to be good at the beginning of a relationship when it's new, fun, and exciting, I'm past the point of worrying about that. Now the only thing really holding me back from telling the people I care about that he and I are seeing each other is the fact that I feel like I've been deceiving them.

"All right, we're all set," Tanner says, getting down off the ladder, and I hold my breath. Honestly it seems like the massive beam now in the ceiling should be held up by more than a few nails and pure physics. "Now we just need to patch up the ceiling and the walls; then we will be done."

"How long do you think that will take?" Cybil asks, and he shrugs.

"We'll get the drywall placed today along with the first layer of mud. Tomorrow we'll make sure there isn't another layer of mud needed, and if there's not, then we'll start to paint," he tells her as she walks to the temporary plastic sheet between the coffee shop and store and pulls it aside to peek between the spaces.

"Can I tell Liam that he can open the store tomorrow?" I ask Tanner but feel Maverick's gaze on me.

"I'd say it would be best to give it one more day. We're going to have to do a lot of sanding, and even with the sheet between stores now, there's still going to be a lot of dust in the air."

"Okay, I'll let him know." I pull out my cell phone and snap a picture of the work the guys completed and then send it to Liam, along with a text letting him know that it's going to be another day yet before he'll be able to open back up again.

"What's the plan for tonight? I was thinking that we could all meet up at the end of the evening," Blake says, looking at the group of us girls.

"No boys are allowed," Margret tells her brother, waving one freshly manicured hand out toward him, and he glowers at her.

This morning Cybil and I left Claire with my mom and went to meet Everly and Margret for manicures and pedicures. Before we met up, the plan was for all of us to spend the entire day together. But while we were getting our nails done, Everly mentioned that Sam wasn't feeling great due to teething, so she didn't want to leave him all day with her mom and would feel better if we all went our separate ways, then met back up this evening for dinner before going out for a couple of hours. Still, sometime between the salon and all of us heading home, we somehow ended up here to watch the guys finish placing the beam in the ceiling.

"I think all of us meeting up at the end of the night sounds like a great idea," Everly says, ignoring Margret.

"It's settled then." Blake smiles smugly at his sister, then kisses his soon-to-be wife. "Where are you heading now?" he asks her.

"I'm going to pick up Sam from my mom," she tells him, causing him to frown. "I don't feel good about leaving him for so long when he's not feeling his best."

"Babe, you know your mom would call if he needed you."

"I know, but I would feel better if he was with me."

"No, you go out with your girls. I'll pick him up from your mom and take him home. He and I can hang together," he tells her softly, and her entire body melts against him.

"Thank you, but I also kind of want to take a nap, so I can do that with him."

"Are you sure?" he asks, and she nods.

"All right." He wraps an arm around her waist and kisses her forehead.

"Are you guys going to be here long?" Cybil asks Tanner, walking over to him for a kiss.

"A couple of hours. We want to get the rest of the shelves painted so that you girls can start getting things set up."

"All right, well, I think Jade and I are going to head back to the house to hang out with Mom for a while before we need to get ready for this evening."

"I should be home before you leave." He kisses her.

"All right, we'll let you guys get back to work." Cybil lets him go, and I go to give my dad a hug, then pull back to look at him.

"Thanks for helping out with everything, Dad."

"You're welcome." He gives me a squeeze, then lets me go, and I turn toward Maverick and bite the inside of my cheek when I find him watching me with his fist clenched.

"Later," I whisper, and he lifts his chin ever so slightly. I know I shouldn't be happy about the fact that he seems to be having some type of internal battle, but it does make me feel better to know I'm not alone in my feelings. I think that both of us are about ready to crack under the pressure of keeping things between us quiet, and really, I don't know which one of us is going to break first. I do know that the two of us are going to have a whole slew of questions to answer when it does happen.

Sitting at the counter in Cybil's kitchen, I smile as I watch my mom, who is sitting on the couch with Claire on her lap, the two of them laughing as my mom sings a song that I can remember from my childhood. As she claps Claire's hands together and rocks her back on her knees, Claire giggles, the sound making me long to have a moment just like this, watching my mom with my own child.

Before my mom had a heart attack, I always thought I would have forever with her; there was never a time limit. Now I know that at the drop of a hat either of my parents could be taken from me, and as much as I hate knowing that, it's made me appreciate the time I have with them so much more.

"Okay, I think I'm ready to go." Cybil steps into the kitchen wearing a pair of dark jeans, a tight cream top with flowy sleeves, and brown pointy-toed bootees with a high heel on her feet that match the material tied around her waist.

"You look amazing." I scoot off my stool, then smooth my hands down the front of my jeans before I walk to where I slipped off my pumps and put them back on.

"Me? Look at you." She comes over as I adjust my top, which might be pointless. There is no real way with the deep V-neck cut of my bodysuit to avoid cleavage, but I also don't want my boobs hanging out all night.

"You both look beautiful." Mom stands with Claire and comes to join us. "So what is the plan for the evening?"

"We're going out to dinner; then after we eat, I think we're going to one of the local bars. Really, Margret hasn't told us much," Cybil says, taking Claire when the baby reaches for her. "I'll have my phone on if you need me for anything."

"We'll be just fine," Mom says, holding her hands out to Claire, and not surprisingly she goes right back to her. "You two just have fun."

"It will probably be an early night." I slip on my jacket and grab my bag off the counter.

"Stay out as long as you want."

"Long gone are the days of us partying all night." I kiss her cheek. "Hopefully Dad will be here soon to keep you company."

"I'm pretty sure that your dad is holding Tanner hostage." She shakes her head. "He wants to help him and the guys get as much work done as he can before we have to go back home."

"Yeah, well, I would like to spend some time with you guys. It's been a whirlwind since you arrived, and I feel like I've barely seen either of you, especially Dad."

Her face softens. "Tomorrow I'll make sure that he doesn't make any plans in the morning, and we can all have breakfast together."

"That sounds like a plan." I lean in to kiss Claire's cheeks, making her laugh, then head for the door as Cybil says goodbye.

Twenty minutes later we pull into the parking lot of the steak house Everly chose for dinner, and as we exit the car, Cybil and I get a text from Margret letting us know that she and Everly have already been seated at the back of the restaurant. When we get inside, we bypass the podium in the front and walk through the dimly lit room to a curved booth in the back, the scent of grilled steak making my stomach growl.

"Were you waiting long?" I ask, arriving at the table and slipping off my jacket so that I can hang it on a hook next to our booth.

"No, I sent the text as soon as we were seated." Margret pats the bench next to her in a silent demand for me to sit down, and I smile as I slide in to sit next to her.

"How was Sam feeling?" Cybil asks Everly as she takes a seat next to her.

"Of course he was fine." She laughs, picking up the drink menu from the middle of the table. "When we got home, he refused to sleep, so we went to the park, which might work out better for my mom, since he will probably go to bed a little earlier than he normally does."

"Is she keeping him overnight?"

"She is." She passes the drink menu to Cybil, who looks at it for a minute before passing it to me. After deciding on a lemon-drop martini, I hand the menu to Margret, then look at the dinner menu on the table. I'm actually starved after not eating much of a lunch today.

"So I brought us some stuff," Margret says a few minutes later after our waiter has walked away with our drink orders.

"Oh Lord," Everly whispers as Margret pulls a large crown out of a black bag and passes it over to her soon-to-be sister-in-law. "You want me to wear this?"

"I don't want you to; you have to wear it." Margret takes it from her and places it on her head. That's when I notice the pink, penis-shaped gems that are incorporated into the design of it.

"I love it." Cybil laughs, and then Margret pulls out three smaller versions of the same crown.

"Well, this gives a new definition to the word *dickhead*," I mumble, taking the crown from her and placing it on my head, and the girls laugh.

"Now these." She pulls out of her bag a white sash with *Bride-to-Be* in gold and places it over Everly's head, pinning it in place.

"Now you two." She gives me one that is black stating that I'm single for the night and another to Cybil with *Hot Mama* on it before she puts on hers, which says *Maid of Dishonor.* "One more thing." She gets out straws that look like penises and places them in our glasses of water.

"Do you have anything else in there?" Everly asks, trying to peek into the bag, but Margret waves her away.

"No, everything else is waiting for us at the bar."

"Should I be worried?" Everly asks, and I laugh at the nervous look she passes around the table.

"Maybe." Margret pats her hand, which is resting on top of the table, then adds, "Just kidding. It's going to be fun."

~

"I don't know that your idea of fun and mine are the same," Everly says a little over an hour and a half later as we enter one of the local bars in town. With Margret leading the way across the mostly empty room, we head to a table that is surrounded by dozens and dozens of floating, brightly colored penis-shaped balloons. A penis-shaped centerpiece with gold streamers shooting out of the tip sits in the middle of the table.

"Did you think you'd get away without having penises at your bachelorette party?" Margret asks, wrapping her arm around Everly's shoulder.

"I hoped I would." Everly laughs. "I'm just happy that there are no strippers."

"Oh, but the night is young, sweet friend," Margret says, making Cybil and me laugh while Everly turns bright pink. "I'm just kidding. My brother told me he would kill me if I hired a stripper, and for once I actually believed him." She sets her bag down on one of the chairs, then walks across the room.

"Should I hide?" Everly asks as Margret goes to the bar and talks to the bartender, who smiles and laughs before bending to get something from the floor at their feet.

"Run," I say, watching a life-size blow-up doll that looks like a man wearing nothing but jeans, boots, and a cowboy hat float over the bar.

"Darn, I really should have listened to you," Everly whispers as Margret marches across the room toward us carrying the fake man with a wide smile on her face.

"This, my beautiful soon-to-be sister-in-law, is your half-naked man for the night." She passes the blow-up doll to Everly, who takes it with no other choice and holds it against her chest. "Now what do you want to drink?"

"Something really, really strong," Everly says, taking a seat on one of the chairs around the table with her fake man sitting across her lap.

Chapter 17

MAVERICK

"We should have come sooner," Blake says as we step inside the bar Margret told us she and the girls would be at.

"Is that a blow-up doll?" Tanner asks, as a life-size plastic man floats over the tops of the girls' heads as they dance in a circle in the middle of a crowded room.

"I'm going to marry that girl," I absently hear Mason say as I track Jade across the room and watch her smile while she sings along with the song that is playing. Her cheeks are pink from dancing, her body outlined by the tight shirt and jeans she is wearing, while her arms float over her head. Beautiful.

"Let's let the girls have a little more fun and grab a beer before we let them know we're here." Tanner pats me on my back, and I drag my attention off Jade and lift my chin.

"I'm gonna guess that my sister is responsible for this," Blake says a few minutes later as we head across the room to the table that is surrounded by a multitude of penises.

"She really stuck with the theme." Mason laughs as Margret spots us and breaks away from the crowd to come join us. The glittery penis crown on her head is half hanging off.

"You're here." She falls against Mason, wrapping her arms around his neck before giving him a kiss and picking up one of the drinks that was left on the table.

"You're not drinking that." He takes it from her before she can put it to her lips, and she pouts.

"I'm not even that drunk."

"You are that drunk, but that's not why you're not drinking it. Someone could have put something in it while you were out dancing." He frowns at her. "I hope you girls haven't been leaving your drinks alone, then coming back to them."

"This is the first time I've been back to the table. Jade was over here earlier, but I don't know if she was drinking what was left of her drink," she says, sounding concerned, and I search the dance floor for Jade and find her, Everly, and Cybil together, laughing and singing as they dance to the new song that is playing.

"Let's get some fresh drinks for you and your girls." Mason leads Margret to the bar.

"I'm going to rescue my fiancée." Blake gets up and heads out to the dance floor, where he wraps his arms around Everly's waist. At first she looks about ready to turn around and kick some ass, but as soon as she finds him, her face lights up, and she spins to face him, wrapping her arms around his neck.

"Are you going to go rescue Cybil?" I ask Tanner, and he shakes his head no.

"She needs this," he says softly with his gaze on his wife across the room. "A few minutes to just be herself with her best friend."

I turn to watch the two of them and smile as they grab the blow-up doll and place it between them to dance with it. Then I go still when a man walks up behind Jade and gets close to her back, wrapping his hand around her hip.

"Easy, man," Tanner says, and I hold steady as a man stands way too fucking close to my woman while she makes it obvious that she's not interested. When she turns away from him and he reaches around her, grasping her breast roughly, I move, making it across the room in four steps.

"What the fuck?" the guy yells, stumbling to the side and tripping over his own feet when I shove him away from her.

"Come on." I hold out my hand toward Jade and wiggle my fingers.

"Maverick," she whispers, her eyes wide as they scan my face.

"What the fuck, man?" is growled from behind me. Then arms go around my waist, and I'm lifted off the ground.

"Put him down," Jade screams, running toward us with the blow-up doll, its size compared to her almost comical. With one move I get free, but before I can fully turn to face the guy who had his arms around me, Cybil kicks him in the nuts, taking him down to his knees, and Jade starts to hit him with the blow-up doll even as he curls into a ball.

"I don't know if I should help or if I should laugh my ass off," Mason mutters, and I shake my head at him while Tanner grabs Cybil around the waist and starts dragging her, kicking and screaming, off the dance floor.

With a shake of my head, I grab the doll from Jade before she can pummel the poor idiot some more, then toss it across the room. "Let's go," I order, and her eyes meet mine before they roam over my face.

"You look mad."

"I am," I tell her truthfully as I hold out my hand. "Let's go."

"You can't be mad at me. I didn't do anything."

"Let's fucking go," I growl, and she steps closer, getting up on her tiptoes, placing her face an inch from mine.

"Do not curse at me, Maverick."

"Then fucking listen to me, Jade." I glare down at her, pissed at myself for not handling that situation better, pissed at her for being so fucking beautiful that men want her, and pissed in general that she's not even mine to claim.

Getting toe to toe with me, she places her finger against my chest. "I don't have—" She doesn't finish; I sink my fingers into her hair, cover her mouth with mine, and thrust my tongue between her lips, cutting off her words. Her arms wrap around my shoulders on instinct, and her breasts press against my chest as I kiss her, not giving a fuck who is around us to witness it.

"The cops are coming," someone yells, and I rip my mouth off Jade's. My chest feels strange as I look down into her pretty eyes, which seem more brown than hazel right now.

"We should go." Tanner walks over with Cybil.

"Yeah, and you and I have a lot to talk about," Cybil tells Jade while handing her her bag and jacket.

"We'll meet you outside," Mason says, walking past us holding Margret's hand.

"Where is Blake?" I ask, then feel a hand on my shoulder.

"I'm right here." He walks around us, heading to the door with his arm around Everly's waist. We follow everyone out the entrance of the bar and head across the parking lot toward where Tanner and I parked, since we were the only two who drove, knowing the girls would each be in their own cars, besides Cybil and Jade.

"I would like to just point out that the whole fight-and-police-being-called business was not my fault," Margret says, and then her eyes go to Jade. "Did I imagine it, or did you really beat that guy with a shirtless cowboy blow-up doll?"

"That totally happened." Cybil laughs. "And he deserved it. What kind of guy just walks up to a woman and gropes her?" She shakes her head in disgust. "I'm glad I kicked him in the nuts—he totally deserved that."

"You girls are lucky you weren't hurt," Tanner tells his wife, not finding the situation as funny as she does. Then again, who knows what might have happened. That guy was at least twice the size of Cybil and

Jade, so if he had decided to put his hands on either of them, they could have been seriously injured.

"Yes, we are, but he still deserved what he got." Cybil shrugs, then looks at her husband. "Do you think we can stop to get breakfast food?"

"Oh, pancakes sound delicious," Everly says, and I look down at Jade.

"I could definitely eat," Jade agrees.

"We might as well go out to eat, since we can't go back into the bar, and there's nowhere else for us to be," Margret says.

"Thank you," Everly tells her, grabbing her hand.

"And while we're there, we can talk about the fact that Maverick and Jade have obviously been seeing each other and keeping it from all of us." Margret grins.

"We are not talking about that," I tell her, and she smiles at me like *Sure, whatever you say*.

"How long has it been going on? Since the first time you met or since you moved here?" Margret keeps going just like the annoying little sister that she is.

"It's none of your business," Blake tells her, and she rests her hands on her hips.

"I think as a family we all should know everything about each other."

"And I think that if Mav and Jade want us to know, they will talk to us," Mason tells her, then opens the passenger-side door of her car for her. "Get in, babe, so that we can go get some food, then head home early."

"This is our first night out in forever, and you want to go home early." She looks up at him, pouting out her bottom lip, and he shakes his head.

"Your parents are watching Taylor. That means we got the house to ourselves when we get home."

"Oh." Her eyes widen and fill with understanding. "Right, let's hurry up and eat, then get home."

Laughing, he shuts the door, then looks around the group. "Meet you all there."

I lift my chin and open the passenger door of my truck, helping Jade into her seat before I shut the door. Really, I'm surprised that she's not arguing with me about leaving her car; then again, she might know that she is in no shape to drive. "Meet you guys at the restaurant," I tell Tanner and Blake as I open the driver's door.

"You kissed me in front of everyone," Jade whispers as I start the engine, and I look over at her.

"I did."

I watch her chew on the inside of her cheek, then let out a deep breath. "They know about us now."

"They already knew about us." I pull out of the lot behind Mason. "Or at least Margret and the guys did."

"You told them?"

"Margret saw me kiss you the first time, and Tanner saw me drive down to your place a few times, so he knew something was up."

"And Blake?"

"That was Tanner gossiping like a high school prom queen."

"Wow, so here I am thinking that I have a big secret, and yet everyone already knew."

"Are you upset they know?"

"No." She gets quiet, and I look over at her, finding that she is nibbling on her bottom lip. "I just hope that Cybil is not upset that I didn't tell her when I normally tell her everything."

"I think she'll understand." I reach over and take her hand. "And I gotta tell you, babe, I'm not upset that I don't have to keep pretending like I don't want to touch you. Not being able to kiss you or hold you when we've been in the same space around our friends has been a special kind of torture."

"I definitely agree with you about that." She gives my fingers a squeeze, then wraps her pinkie around mine. "Remember when we promised that we would stay friends or at least friendly if this ends," she says softly.

"I remember." I glance over at her, not liking that pain in the center of my chest even one little bit.

"That still stands, right?"

"That still stands, baby. No matter what happens, we'll be friends."

"Okay." She turns to look out the window. As much as I want to push her to tell me what she's thinking, I don't, because I have no desire to be her friend. I want to be a whole lot more than that.

Lying awake with Jade curled against my side, her head resting on my chest and her leg over my hip, I stare at the ceiling.

Since I can remember, I've done everything to avoid this kind of intimacy with a woman. I've kept very strict rules when dating, making sure to always keep my distance and never let a woman close.

Jade is the first woman I let in and wanted more from, and with her it seems even when she gives me more, it's still not enough. I don't need a psychologist to tell me that my mom being in and out of my life for years before completely jumping ship fucked me up.

She was young when she and my dad met, just sixteen when she had my sister, and when she got pregnant with me, she and my dad were not even together. She had been in town to see Lizzy and wound up with another child she didn't really want. And soon after I was born, she dropped me off at my dad's, and she didn't show up again until after I was two; then every few years she'd drop by, sometimes for just a few days, others for months at a time. I loved having her around. She was fun, beautiful, and for short bursts of time, she made it seem like we had the perfect family. Then she'd leave, and we'd all crash from the high and end up moving to a new place, which was probably my dad's way of trying to start over. It was a fucked-up roller coaster for everyone, especially for me as a little kid.

It wasn't until I was around thirteen that I realized how wrong what she was doing was, but I didn't have a say, and my dad would never cut her off. He loved her, and I imagine he still does, even if he's never said it. Then again, actions speak louder than words, and him never having another relationship is loud as fuck. Me? I cut her off when I was nineteen, the first and last time she showed up at where I was stationed and asked to stay for a few days, only to take the cash I had been saving up for a house and leave without so much as a *fuck you*. Lizzy, on the other hand, has let our mother float in and out of her life, claiming that she wants the boys to know their grandmother. She's made of stronger stuff than I am.

Coming out of my head when Jade's cell starts to ring on the nightstand, I listen to her groan right before her hand moves to my stomach and she pushes up, moving her hair out of her face.

"Morning." I smile, and she narrows her eyes on mine.

"It's really not fair that you look like you do in the morning when I'm sure I look like I got hit by a car," she says.

I lift my hand to smooth my fingers down her cheek.

"You look beautiful, even hungover."

"You're a liar, but whatever," she grumbles, and I laugh as she moves to get her phone, which has quit ringing. When she turns to get on her knees so that she can reach it on the other side of the bed, I smooth my hand over the curve of her round ass.

"Oh no," she cries suddenly, and my muscles tighten.

"What?"

"I'm supposed to be at breakfast." She turns around to face me, shoving her phone close to my face. "Mom left a message telling me that breakfast is at ten. It's ten now." She drops her phone, then rolls off the bed, searching the floor.

"Your jeans are in the kitchen."

"In the kitchen?" She looks at the door, and I grin.

"On the way home, you told me in the truck that you were going to rock my world. When we got here, you started stripping down as soon as we walked through the door. Then you passed out as soon as your ass hit the mattress."

"Oops." She fiddles with the bottom of the T-shirt I put on her last night, and I laugh.

"It's all good." I get off the bed and stop to kiss her before I ask, "Do you want a piece of toast and some Tylenol?"

"That would probably be good." She follows me out of the room to the kitchen, where she grabs her jeans off the stool and puts them on.

"Remind me to never drink mimosas again."

"Not sure it was the mimosas that did you in, baby. Pretty sure that was just the icing on the cake." I put two pieces of bread in the toaster, then grab a glass, fill it with water, and hand it to her.

"Thank you." She takes a seat on the stool and takes a sip, then rests her hand on her stomach. After I butter the toast, I pass it over to her, then go to the cupboard and grab the pill bottle, take out two, and give them to her.

"Feeling nauseous?" I get close and rest my hand on her belly, and she covers it with her own.

"A little. I don't know how Cybil dealt with being nauseous for months when she first got pregnant." A strange sensation fills my chest, and I move my hand and take a step back.

"Eat, and I'll drive you up to Tanner's place."

"Are you going to stay for breakfast with my parents?" she asks, and I hold her gaze for a long moment. Weeks ago I would have said no. Now? Fuck me, I'm in over my head, and I knew I would be the moment I walked up to her car in the middle of a snowstorm and she rolled down her window.

"Do you want me there?"

"Yes." She nibbles her bottom lip like she's nervous.

"Then I'll be there." I lean in to give her a quick kiss, then head for the bedroom, saying over my shoulder, "While you eat, I'll get dressed."

"Okay, just so you know, I'm stealing your shirt."

"I'll get it back from you later."

"You won't; it's mine now." I stop to look at her in my kitchen with her hair a mess around her shoulders and her face still soft from sleep and know right then and there that a lot more than my tee is hers now.

"Yeah, I guess it is." I rub my chest, and she gives me a smug smile before taking a bite of toast. Yeah, I'm fucked.

Chapter 18

JADE

"Those boys of yours sure are handsome," Mom whispers as she, Cybil, and I stand outside the store and watch Maverick and Tanner help Dad unload all the boxes from the back of his truck and carry them into the store.

Maybe not surprisingly, Mom and Dad were both thrilled to find out about Maverick and me, especially since they already know and like him. And Cybil shockingly didn't seem even a little bothered that I had kept Maverick and me a secret. She said while we got a few minutes alone yesterday after breakfast that she'd guessed that there was something going on between us but that she'd figured I was working through my feelings and would talk to her about it when I was ready.

Obviously my best friend is a better person than I am, because I think I would have been in a snit at least for a few days if I found out she was keeping something that big from me. Then again, she probably knows me better than anyone else, which is not only why she understood that I needed time to come to terms with what was happening between Maverick and me but also why she was so insistent on me moving to Montana in the first place. She knew that I would find what she had here. A place where I'm not only accepted for who I am but surrounded by people who are just good people who want the best for me.

"They really are," Cybil agrees just as quietly, and Claire giggles her agreement. "Okay, enough drooling. We have work to do." Cybil heads into the store carrying Claire, and I walk in behind her and Mom, then put down Claire's walker, which she doesn't walk in yet, since she's not quite big enough to move around on her feet, even though she wants to be. As soon as I set it up, Cybil places Claire in it, and she starts to bounce and make music with the buttons that light up.

"So tell me what you want me to do," Mom says as Maverick walks in, his eyes meeting mine, and my stomach flutters when he winks as he sets down the stack of boxes he is holding. I drag my eyes off him, then look around at all the boxes already stacked up against the walls.

"I say we just start unpacking books and getting them on shelves." I carefully open one of the boxes closest to me and pull out a stack of books that all have the same title. "Once we have everything unpacked, I'll go back through and organize." I look at Cybil. "When are the girls going to start bringing their stuff over?"

"I think today and tomorrow." She opens another box and starts helping me stack books while Claire giggles and dances to the music. "Do you want us to try and set up the register today?"

"We should. We also need to talk about the opening." I look at the plastic sheet that is still taped up between the stores even though all the work has been completed. "I know that Everly invited me to the lake house for the wedding and the weekend, but with all the stuff happening here, I don't feel comfortable being gone for that long. I'm thinking that I'll head up Saturday night so that I'll be there for the wedding Sunday; then Monday, if you agree, we can have a soft opening, get all the kinks worked out throughout the week, then have the grand opening Friday. And maybe when we close, we can have a small party here with the girls who are going to have their stuff in the store, along with all of our friends and family."

"I love that idea, but I don't want you to stay here working while we're all up at the lake house relaxing and having fun." She looks around. "And really I think that we should be able to get everything done and set up this week so we can all leave Friday."

"I don't mind staying behind if I have to," I say, and she rests her shoulder against mine.

"I know that you don't. I also know you were used to doing everything on your own at your shop, but you're not alone here. This place is just as much my responsibility as it is yours. We'll get everything done this week; then we'll take a few days off before we open this place up. Okay?"

"Okay," I agree, and she nudges me with her shoulder. Then, for the next few hours, we open boxes and put stuff on the shelves while Maverick and Tanner work on setting up the register for us and Claire plays with the ever-growing pile of empty boxes.

And as I step out onto the sidewalk later that evening with Maverick waiting for me, I take one last look at the space before I flip off the light. There is still a whole lot to be done, but it is already better than I even envisioned it could be. Really, my whole life is better than I envisioned it could be, I think as I take Maverick's hand and walk down the sidewalk at his side.

~

With my head pillowed on Maverick's biceps, I wake when I feel him move behind me. I turn my head to try and look at him over my shoulder through the dark.

"You're not leaving, are you?" I ask him, and his hand on my hip slides up ever so slightly, then moves across my belly and under the waistband of my shorts.

"No." He presses his hips forward into my ass, and his cock throbs against my backside.

"Oh," I whisper as my stomach muscles contract and my core clenches at the reminder of what it's like having him inside me.

"Maverick," I breathe as his fingers slip lower over my pubic bone, then down between the lips of my sex. On instinct I rock into his hand, wanting more of his touch, and he nips the back of my neck while his fingers freeze.

"Hold still." I do: my muscles tighten, my breath gets trapped in my lungs, and I wait for his next move, knowing it will be worth it for me in the end. "Good girl." He skims two fingers over my clit, and I bite back a moan as I become even wetter.

"Oh God." I let out a whimpered breath as his fingers slip lower.

"You're already fucking soaked." His warm breath brushes the back of my neck, and then he slides one, then two fingers inside me. My thighs tremble as he plays with me, his fingers rubbing against a spot deep inside me while the heel of his palm presses against my clit. As tends to happen when he touches me, I'm soon, maybe too soon, fighting the urge to come. Reaching behind me, I grasp his cock before he can stop me and slide my hand down the length over his boxers.

I listen to him groan and then gasp when he pulls his fingers from me and rolls me to my back. I focus on his face, the only light coming from one of those plug-in night-lights on the wall. As he lowers his head toward mine, I lean up to kiss him, but he shakes his head while lifting his chin.

"Lift your ass." I do, and he tugs my thin cotton shorts down my legs and tosses them to the floor. "Now open your legs." I do, after hesitating for a half a second, and as his mouth covers mine, his hand slips back between my legs. His tongue slides into my mouth, and two fingers fill me, causing my back to arch and a loud moan to leave my mouth. My nails dig into his biceps as he works his fingers in and out of me, each thrust creating a tightening sensation in my lower belly.

Needing to touch him, I move my hand to his chest, then slide it down under the edge of his boxers so that I can wrap my hand around his silky length, which pulses against my palm.

"I'm so close." I lean up, and he kisses me as he uses my wetness to circle my clit. Just like that I fall over the edge into an orgasm that takes my breath and traps his hand between my legs. As I come, he covers my hand with his on his length and pumps. I open my eyes, wanting to watch him lose himself but needing him inside of me more. "I want you," I pant, my chest rising and falling quickly.

"I only had the one condom we used last night when we got here." He pumps faster, and I lick my lips.

"I'm on birth control," I whisper, and he stills completely. I don't even think he takes a breath.

"Jade."

"And I'm clean."

"Fuck," he growls. Then he's off the bed, and I think I said something wrong. He stares at me for a long moment, then shucks off his boxers before he comes back to me, helping me to sit up so that he can help me take off my tank top before he places his hand on my belly, pushing me back to lie on the bed as he falls between my thighs. "I'm clean."

"I trust you." I wrap my legs around his hips and grab hold of his shoulders as he takes hold of his length and presses against my entrance. I listen to his breath hitch at the contact and swallow hard as my throat burns. This moment feels bigger than just sex, more important than the two of us not using a condom. A niggle of worry fills the back of my mind, but before I can catch the reason for it, he's thrusting inside of me.

Filled with him, feeling all of him, I lift my head, and he kisses me, his movements slow and steady, our bodies moving in sync as he makes love to me. "Do you know how good you feel?" he asks, pulling his mouth from mine to rest his forehead against mine. "Like silk and home, everything fucking good." He swivels his hips, and I clench around him. "Damn, baby, I never thought that you could feel better, but I was wrong, so fucking wrong." He picks up speed, moving his hand between us, rolling his fingers over my clit. My core clenches tight as heat spreads through me like a tidal wave, and I lift my head, biting down on his shoulder as I come, hearing him curse. After slamming his hips into mine three more times, he bottoms out deep inside me and falls against my chest, then rolls us so that I'm sprawled out against his chest, which is rising and falling quickly.

"I bit you," I tell him, sounding out of breath and as sleepy as I feel.

"I know." His chest moves like he's laughing.

"I'm sorry?" Honestly, I've never done something like that before; then again, no man has ever brought out the emotions in me that he has.

"Don't apologize. You can bite me any fucking time you like." He kisses the top of my head, and I smile as my eyes start to get heavy.

"I should go clean up."

"Not yet." He holds me tight, then pulls a blanket over us. "I like you like this."

"I like being with you like this," I admit, letting my eyes slide closed. As I lie there, listening to the steady beat of his heart, I try to decipher exactly what the emotion is that's sitting in the middle of my chest. It doesn't feel like anything I've ever felt before; it's light and heavy but warm and comforting. It's not love—I know that I've felt that emotion a time or two before. I just hope that whatever it is, he's feeling it too.

"My sister called me this afternoon. She asked if I was heading down to her for Thanksgiving," he says into the dark, breaking the comfortable silence between us, and I move my head to rest my chin on his chest.

"Are you?"

"Yeah, but I'd like you to go with me," he says, and my heart pounds. I know he told me that he wanted me to meet his sister and her family when they came for the New Year in a few months, but that was a long ways off. I also know without him telling me that him want-ing me to meet his sister is huge. She's the woman who basically raised him after his mother left, and he's the man he is today because of her.

"I'd like that. I'll talk to Cybil and see what we can work out for the store; maybe one of the other ladies who are working with us will be willing to cover the store while I'm out of town." I rest my cheek back where it was, then ask, "Is your dad going to be there too?"

"No." His fingers, which were moving along my spine, still. "He . . ." He clears his throat. "Neither Lizzy or I see him much. He works a lot."

My chest aches from the pain in his voice, and I wish I knew what to say or do to make it better. But since there are no words to make him feel better, I turn my head to kiss his chest, then whisper, "I'm sorry."

"Thanks, baby," he whispers back, and I hug his waist, then feel his lips rest against the top of my hair. "What time are your dad and your mom leaving to drive home?" he asks, dragging me from my thoughts, and I glance over at the clock on the bedside table.

"Soon. They said six; it's five thirty," I tell him quietly, wishing that their time here wasn't already up and that they were going to be here a little longer. It's been so good having them around, and with them here, I honestly feel like I have everything I need and then some.

"Let's get dressed. It's cold out—I'll drive you up to the house so that you can say goodbye to them."

"Okay," I say quietly, pushing up off his chest and going to the bathroom to clean up before I get dressed in a pair of sweats and a long-sleeved shirt.

After I'm ready, he drives us up to the house, and then Cybil, Tanner, Claire, Maverick, and I say goodbye to my parents. The only thing making the moment a little easier is having Maverick's arms wrapped around me as I cry while watching them drive off, as well as the knowledge that they will be back in a month for another visit.

Chapter 19

JADE

With the sun setting, I watch Blake, Everly, and Sam as they slow dance in the middle of the empty dance floor while a man and woman sing about how they will follow each other no matter where they go in life. Tears fill my eyes, and I quickly grab my napkin to blot under them. Having gotten to know Everly and her sweet son, I couldn't be happier for her and Sam and Blake. They truly make a beautiful family.

"Oh God, I'm going to cry," Cybil whispers, and I turn toward her, finding tears wetting her cheeks.

"You're already crying, Sunshine," Tanner says, moving Claire to his other thigh so that he can pull his wife against his side and kiss her temple.

"They are just so perfect together," she tells him, and I grab her napkin and hand it to her so that she can wipe her face. The good thing is that we are not the only two bawling our eyes out; there doesn't seem to be a dry eye as I look around the tent that we are sitting under. Not that it's the first time I've cried today—I sobbed during their ceremony when Blake's mom handed Sam over to Blake, and he placed a gold bracelet around Sam's tiny wrist as a promise to love him forever as he would love his mom.

"Thank goodness," Tanner mutters when the song changes to one that is more upbeat and the DJ asks others to join the new couple on the dance floor. "I thought I was going to float out onto the lake with all the tears around here."

Hearing Maverick chuckle, I glare at him.

"Sorry, babe, but he's not wrong."

"Whatever, you guys just don't get romance." I roll my eyes at him, and he grins as he squeezes my thigh.

"Now that the waterworks are over, will you dance with me?" Tanner asks as he stands, and Cybil looks between him and Claire, then puts her hand in his, and the three of them head toward the wooden makeshift dance floor.

I watch them as they start to do some kind of chicken dance, then laugh as Claire's giggles of happiness travel around the room. Picking up my glass of wine, I take a sip, then look at Maverick. "Are you having fun?"

"Yeah," he says easily, picking up his beer, and I smile at him, then look to the side when I feel a small hand on my arm.

"Do you want to dance?" a cute little boy with red hair who must be nine or ten asks, and I set down my wineglass.

"I would love to." I look over at Maverick. "Do you want to join us?"

"I'm good, baby. Go on. I'll be here when you get back." He grins, and I grin back, then slide off my seat and take the kid's hand. When we get out onto the dance floor, a song I know starts to play, and I show him how to do the moves that go along with the lyrics. Then one song turns to another, and we dance, sing, and laugh. As I'm in the middle of doing the Macarena, my eyes find Maverick's, and a flutter happens in my chest as our gazes lock across the room.

"Uh-oh." Margret bumps into me with her hip, and I look over at her. "Someone is in love," she shouts over the music and the sound of people laughing and talking.

"What? No." I look at her while I shake my head from side to side.

"You are, honey, but don't worry—so is he." She giggles when Mason spins her around to face him, and my heart pounds as my eyes move to Maverick, who is still watching me with a warm look in his eyes. No way. He doesn't love me. Right?

"I think I'm going to get a drink," my dance partner says, and I look down at his adorable little face, which is red with exertion. "It's been fun."

"Yeah, it has." I watch him walk over to an older woman with long gray hair before I leave the dance floor and go back to the table, Margret's words floating over and over on repeat in my head.

"Did you have fun?" Maverick asks as I take a seat next to him, and I pick up my water glass that was left over from dinner.

"Yes." I smile at him, and his eyes roam my face.

"Should I be worried that you're going to leave me for a younger man?"

"No, I'm all yours." I turn toward him, and he wraps his hand around the back of my neck to drag me forward and kiss me.

"That's good, but you should know that I would fight for you."

"Would you?" I ask him on a whisper as my heart pounds, and he holds our faces just inches apart.

"Yes." He nips my bottom lip, then kisses me again before letting his hand slide away.

"Do you want to dance?" I ask him after picking up my wineglass and drinking the rest of it in two gulps.

"Dancing is not really my thing," he says quietly, lifting my hand to kiss my fingers. "Do you want to go on a walk with me?"

"A walk?"

"Yeah, I'd like to show you something."

"Sure." I set down my glass and stand to take my sweater off the back of my chair. With Blake and Everly's wedding being outdoors, we were told that we would need to bring something warm for when we walked from the house to the heated tent, then to the backyard, then back to the house again when the party was over. Really, I thought that I would have to wear my sweater the entire time, which would suck because my black body-conforming off-the-shoulder dress is too gorgeous to cover up, but with the magic of at least a dozen heat lamps, it's as warm as a summer day under the tent.

After I put on my sweater, Maverick places his hand against my lower back and leads me through the crowd to the exit, and then, hand in hand, we walk toward the dock where Everly and Blake got married earlier today. Only now there are no longer flowers tied to each post along the dock, and it's dark, the moon lighting our path and reflecting off the water while the stars seem to sparkle above us.

"Are we going hunting for the lake monster?" I joke as we walk down the wooden dock, and he laughs, probably remembering the same story I do. A story Everly and Blake told us about how the two of them ended up in the water on their first visit here. Apparently Blake told Everly a story about a monster that supposedly lives in the lake, and Everly was so freaked that when a fish jumped out of the water, she ended up capsizing their canoe.

"No." He wraps his arms around me when we reach the end of the dock, and then he tips his head back to look at the night sky, and I do the same. "Tonight is one of the largest meteor showers in the last twenty years," he tells me, and my fingers grasp his suit jacket while I watch a shooting star streak across the sky. "Make a wish," he whispers.

With my belly fluttering, I close my eyes and make a wish, a wish for my future with this man. A future that is filled with love, a ring, and a baby with his dark hair and beautiful eyes. Normally I would never waste a wish on something that seems so far fetched, but standing in his arms, I can't help but feel like that future for me and for him is something that we could have.

"Did you make a wish?" I ask, opening my eyes and finding him watching me.

"I've already got everything I want," he tells me, and I melt into him. "What did you wish for?" He smooths my hair back away from my face, tucking some behind my ear.

"For that." I wave a hand out toward the tent, which is lit up, with the sound of music and laughter floating from it. "I want what Everly and Blake have, what Tanner and Cybil have found. I want to get married one day and have babies." I lean into him and smile, the alcohol in my system like a dose of truth serum.

"Jade." His voice sounds gruff, and I get up on my tiptoes, moving my hands to his chest.

"Don't worry; I'm not mentally planning our wedding or anything. I just mean that one day I would love to get married and have a family of my own."

"You deserve those things." He presses my cheek to his chest while his chin rests on the crown of my head. Then he holds me like that for a long time as stars shoot across the sky above us. And stupidly I don't realize that even though I'm still standing in his arms, he's a million miles away.

~

"Thank you for inviting me. I had the very best time." I hug Everly and rock her back and forth as we stand on Blake's family's front porch.

"Thank you for coming." She lets me go and grasps my upper arms. "I can't wait to see the store on Friday for the grand opening."

"I can't wait either." I let her go so that I can give Blake a hug, and then I kiss Sam's chubby cheek before I take a step back so Maverick can say goodbye.

"Congrats again, man. I'll see you in a few days," Maverick tells Blake, giving him a one-armed hug before turning to chuck Sam under the chin and then kiss Everly's cheek.

"If you need me, don't call," Blake tells him, and Maverick chuckles.

"I won't," he assures him, and I head down the steps of the front porch with Maverick behind me. I walk to his truck parked at the end of the driveway, then turn to smile and wave at Everly and Blake, watching the two of them laugh.

"Ready?" Maverick opens the passenger door for me to get into my seat, and the weight that has been growing in the pit of my stomach all morning gets a little heavier when he doesn't touch me or kiss me. A weight that started forming first thing this morning, when I woke up without him next to me. I tried not to let my imagination get away from me then, but when I found him in the kitchen with his friends having breakfast, it felt like there was a wall between us that hadn't been there before last night. I don't know what changed, but I know something did.

"Did you have fun this weekend?" I ask him when he gets in behind the wheel, and he glances over at me quickly before placing his hand on the back of my seat and reversing onto the road.

"Yeah," he says easily, and I shift in my seat and wonder if I shouldn't have stayed with Cybil and Tanner and left with them later this afternoon. "Did you have fun?"

"It was a beautiful wedding." I dig through my bag for my cell phone, and once I find it, I send a text to Liam, letting him know that I'm heading back to town. I also let him know that I'll stop by the store this evening to check on things and to make sure we're ready to go for tomorrow morning, when we remove the plastic between the store and coffee shop.

When I'm done, I tuck my phone back into my bag, then turn to stare out the window as we drive back home, trying to figure out what happened between last night and this morning. He seemed fine when we got back to the tent after standing under the stars, or maybe drunk me thought he was fine because I was having a great time with our friends, dancing and enjoying all the wedding festivities.

He also seemed fine when we got back to our room to go to bed. Like he's done since the first time we slept together, he held me against him as I fell asleep. The only thing that was different is we didn't have sex, but then again, I didn't think we would, since I'm on my period, plus I know he's not the kind of guy to be annoyed with not getting lucky, since we've had a few nights together when we didn't have sex. I bite my lip, trying to pinpoint what happened, but know in my gut that without asking him, I might not ever know, and it's obvious that something is bothering him. Figuring asking him is better than shoving open the door and jumping out of the truck, I pull in a deep breath, trying to find the courage to ask him what is going on.

"Are you mad about something?" My question cuts through the silence that has settled over us like a wet blanket for the last hour and a half, and I look over at him, finding his hands wrapped around the steering wheel so tight that his knuckles have turned white.

"I'm not mad, but we should talk," he says, and my heart sinks. God, how many times have I heard that before? *We should talk* is always a prelude to *This isn't working, but don't worry; it's not you, it's me.*

"Okay." I wait, holding my breath for what seems like forever. Then he glances over at me, his expression filled with so much pain that I feel it like it's my own.

"I don't want to get married or to have kids," he says softly, but his tone does nothing to lessen the sudden impact of pain I feel in the center of my chest.

"Is there a reason why you don't want those things?"

"Does there need to be?" He shakes his head, and I want to scream *yes*, but I don't. I somehow manage to keep my mouth closed and the tears forming in the back of my throat at bay. "Can you accept that?"

My first instinct is to say yes because if I do, maybe then I will be able to keep him for a little while longer, but the truth is I do want to get married. I want a baby of my own. I want to watch my parents with my son or daughter, and I really want to experience the kind of love that Cybil, Everly, and Margret have found. And I know that if I lie right now, it will only lead to more heartache later on.

"No." I dig my nails into my palms. "I'm sorry, but no, I can't accept that."

"Yeah, that's what I thought," he whispers while a single tear slides down my cheek. When I see that we are getting close to the center of town, where the coffee shop and the store are, I pick up my bag from the floor, where I rested it near my feet.

"Can you drop me off at the store? I have some work to do there before we open tomorrow."

"How about I take you home and we talk there," he suggests, and my insides seize up.

"What is there to talk about? You just told me that you don't want to get married or have kids." I wipe away another tear quickly. "And I do want those things." *With you,* I leave out. "I don't think we need to have a conversation about that, unless you want to explain to me why you don't want a wife and baby someday." I wait for him to say something, anything, but he doesn't. "Please just drop me off." I place my hand on the door handle, honestly ready to toss myself bodily from his truck if he refuses.

"I'll drop you off and take your bag up to Tanner's," he says, and I nod, wanting to tell him that I don't care what he does with my stuff as long as I'm able to escape his truck and the pain that is spreading from the center of my chest outward, making me feel like I'll crack open at any second.

"Thank you." I wait until he's double-parked on the main street between the coffee shop and store, then fling my door open.

"Jade," he calls, his voice gruff, and I turn to look at him before I hop out. God, even as hurt as I am, I hate seeing pain in his eyes.

"Friends?" I hold out my pinkie, and his eyes drop to my hand between us for a long moment before he wraps his finger tightly around mine. "I'll see you around." I swallow down the tears I can feel building, let him go, and get out like his truck is on fire.

And only once I'm inside the store and tucked away in the bathroom do I let myself cry.

Chapter 20

JADE

"Oh my God, I loved that book you recommended for me to read," a cute little blonde wearing a cheerleader outfit with a cup of coffee in hand gushes as she walks up toward the register where I'm standing. "I mean, I wasn't sure that I would be into elves and magic, but the story sucked me in, and Christen was so hot."

"I'm so glad you enjoyed it." I make sure to keep my smile in place, a smile that has felt forced for the last four days. Then again, my heart was ripped out and stomped on four days ago, and even if I was able to lie to myself about not being in love with Maverick while he and I were together, the pain in my chest is a constant reminder that I'm an idiot and lying to myself did nothing to protect me from heartache.

"Did you see that I got the second book in the series today?" I ask her, wishing that talking about books would make me as happy as it used to.

"I didn't." She spins around, goes to the shelf where the first one is located, and picks up the second one, squealing as she holds it to her chest. "I'm so excited." She comes to the counter with it, reading the back blurb.

"Have you read it yet?" She hands it to me.

"I haven't yet, but it's next on my list. The reviews on it so far are fantastic."

"Well, if it's anything like the first one, I bet they are." She passes me her credit card, and I swipe it through the machine; then, while she plugs in her code, I place her book in a black bag.

"You'll have to come back to let me know how it is." I hand her her purchase, and she smiles.

"I will." She bounces through the opening of the store into the coffee shop, waving at Katie and Tony before she disappears out of sight.

With the store empty, something that doesn't happen very often, I go around and make sure that the books are on the shelves where they should be and that the items that the other girls are selling are in order. Since opening just four days ago, we have already paid our rent for the month and made a small profit. It's been beyond huge having the store attached to the coffee shop, and just like I thought would happen, people are constantly coming in here to look around, either while they wait for their drinks or after they have their coffee in hand. I also love that there are men and women coming in here to purchase books that they might not have purchased otherwise.

When I hear the door ding, letting me know that someone is here, I stand from where I was squatted adjusting a stack of books, then smile when I see Cybil with Claire.

"Hey, I didn't think you were going to be here until later," I say as I take Claire from her and rest her on my hip.

"I know, but Claire woke from her nap a little early, so I thought we would come over to see if there was anything we could do to help get ready for tomorrow," she says, but I know she's lying. She's been worried about me. Everyone has been.

"I don't think so." I shrug. "Balloons are being delivered in the morning, and the people who own the liquor store down the street are dropping off the champagne in the evening, right before we close the door to celebrate. I figured I would just go to the store tonight and pick up the stuff to make a giant charcuterie board that people can pick at and keep it simple."

"You don't have to worry about that. I'll take care of it when I leave here and just keep it in my fridge and bring it with me tomorrow."

"That works for me."

"Awesome." She looks around. "How was today?"

"Good, everyone who's walked through the door has walked out with something, so that's good, right?" I carry Claire to behind the counter, where her bouncer is, and place her in it with one of her toys.

"How are you?" she asks, and I shrug.

"Good."

"Jade." She sighs.

"Please don't," I whisper. "I can't. I don't want to talk about how I'm feeling or anything else. I don't want to cry." *I cry enough at night when I'm lying in bed alone,* I think but don't say.

"Tanner and Blake talked to Maverick."

"Good." I know that Tanner and Blake were both pissed at their friend on my behalf, but I never wanted that, especially knowing how close the three of them are.

"Tanner said Mav is a mess." My heart clenches at that news, and I don't know if I should be happy or sad that he's as messed up as I am. "I guess Tanner called his sister and asked her to come to town to see if she can sort him out."

"Good. It would be good for him to see her; I know he misses her," I say quietly.

"I'm worried about you, Jade," she says, getting close, and I drag in a deep breath.

"I'll be fine. I just need more than a few days to get over him," I say, knowing that's a lie. I don't know if even a lifetime would be long enough to get over Maverick. I thought I knew what heartbreak was, but now I know I was wrong. The pain I've felt the last few days has been overwhelming. And I know that if I didn't care about letting Cybil down, I wouldn't even bother getting out of bed.

"I really thought that you two—"

"Stop." I cut her off before she can finish that sentence. "It is what it is; him and I do not want the same things, and as much as that sucks, I need to accept it. I'm just glad he told me now rather than months down the road, when I'd inevitably be deeper in love with him."

"I guess you're right about that." She looks down at Claire, and I wonder if she's trying to imagine what she would have done if Tanner had told her that he didn't want kids. Thankfully she will never have to find out, because Tanner wants whatever makes her happy, and if she told him that she wanted a dozen kids, he'd happily give them to her.

"Do you think I messed up?" I dig my nails into my palms, and she looks at me.

"What do you mean?"

"You would do anything for Tanner, right? Do you think I messed up by wanting it all from Maverick and not giving him what he wants, which is just me?"

"God, no." She engulfs me in a tight hug. "You did not mess up." She lets me go just enough to look me in the eye. "You deserve it all, Jade, and I would be disappointed if you ever settled for less than that." I watch tears fill her eyes. "One day you are going to be a wife and a mom, and when that happens, all of this will be worth it."

"I miss him," I admit as my eyes start to burn.

"I know you do, and I wish that I could take the pain you're feeling right now. I hate that you are hurting." She pulls me in for another hug. "And you don't know what the future holds for the two of you; this could just be a bump in the road."

"I don't think this is a bump, and if I've learned anything over the years, it's that men don't normally say things they don't mean, so if Maverick says he doesn't want kids, he doesn't want them," I say, letting her go.

"You saw him with Claire. He adores her."

"I know, and he also loves his nephews, but that doesn't change anything."

"Men are idiots sometimes."

"I won't disagree with you about that." I smile when she laughs and wipe at the tears on my cheeks.

"You know, whatever happens, I'm here for you, and so is Tanner and everyone else, right?"

"I know, and one day when I don't hurt so much, I hope that I can get back to being friends with Maverick so no one will feel uncomfortable having the two of us around at the same time."

"No one is going to feel uncomfortable." She shakes her head, then adds, "Well, Maverick might when I kick his ass for hurting you, but I think even he'd agree that he deserves it."

"You couldn't hurt a fly." I pick up Claire when she starts to babble "Jada," which she uses only when I'm around, so I've assumed she's calling for me.

"I'll have you know I've taken down a grown man in a bar fight before," she says, and I laugh at her. "Don't laugh. I'm serious."

"I know you are. I was there," I agree, then look toward the doorway, seeing none other than Donna, Ken the cop's wife, walk in. As she gets closer, I know instantly that she did not take him back; she looks refreshed, like she's been at the spa for a month, or like the weight of a worthless two-hundred-pound man is no longer hanging around her shoulders.

"Donna," I greet, and she looks surprised that I remember her name, when, really, how could I forget it?

"Hi, I . . ." She looks between Cybil and me. "Is now a good time to talk?"

"Sure," I say, figuring that even if she wants to talk about Ken, that will be better than spending more time talking or thinking about Maverick.

"I know that when I saw you last and you offered me a job, you were probably just doing it to be nice, but I figured it wouldn't hurt to stop in here and see about picking up an application."

"I wasn't saying it to be nice," I tell her, then introduce her to Cybil. "This is my best friend, Cybil; she and I own this place," I tell her, then add: "I don't have any applications right now, but if you want, we can go over the job we'd hire you for and see if it's something you'd be interested in." After Cybil and I worked the first two days, we both agreed that we would need to hire on another girl, and since all the women who have stuff in the shop are pretty busy most of the time, we knew we needed to hire from outside.

"Will I be making money?" she asks, and I nod. "Then it's the job I want."

"Have you ever worked retail before?" Cybil asks her, and she shrugs.

"I've worked in a couple of clothing stores and a fast-food place before; does that count?"

"That counts," Cybil says, and I notice Donna watching me closely.

"I don't want to intrude, and I know it's not my place, but it looks like you've been crying."

"Guy trouble," I admit, and her face gets soft.

"Sorry."

"It happens, right?" I ask, and she shrugs one shoulder.

"It used to happen to me all the time; then I found Ken out at dinner with you and kicked him to the curb. Since then, no more guy trouble, and I feel happier than I have in a couple of years."

"Wait, you're the cop's wife?" Cybil asks, and Donna focuses on her.

"Soon-to-be ex-wife, but yes."

"You're hired." Cybil grins at her, and Donna laughs. "No, I'm serious," Cybil says, looking at me. "Right?"

"Absolutely, if you want a job here, it's yours."

"I'll take it," she says, so Cybil and I go over what we would expect, which isn't much more than checking people out and making sure things stay tidy around the shop. And Donna tells us that she's familiar with the computer system we use, which will make it that much easier to get her trained.

By the time she leaves, I'm wondering if Ken is kicking his own ass for doing a woman like Donna wrong. I hope he is; I hope he goes to bed at night wishing he would have done everything to keep her, and if I'm honest, I hope that Maverick goes to bed every night wishing the same thing.

Chapter 21

MAVERICK

"Wake up, you idiot," someone yells while banging something. I jolt awake and flip on the bedside lamp, finding my sister across the room banging a wooden spoon against the back of one of the metal pots from my kitchen.

"Lizzy, what the fuck?" I rub my face, then push my hair back as I sit up.

"Don't 'what the fuck' me, you idiot." She sends the wooden spoon flying through the air in my direction, and I just barely catch it before it hits me in the head. "I got a call from Tanner."

Fuck.

I should have known he'd call her; he and Blake have both been all over my ass the last few days, trying to sort out my shit, and I know they are worried.

"Lizzy."

"He told me that you broke up with the first girl you've ever fallen in love with."

"I never told you I was in love with her." I toss back the blanket that is over me and get out of bed.

"You had her in your house. You told me you wanted to bring her to Thanksgiving to meet me and the boys. You didn't have to tell me you were in love with her with words, you idiot; you spelled it out in black and white with actions."

"Yeah, well, things change," I mutter, grabbing a pair of my sweats and putting them on.

"Why's that?"

"Because she and I do not want the same things."

"You didn't want the same things? What does that even mean?"

"I don't want a wife or kids." I move past her, giving her a wide berth so I don't end up smacked upside the head, and walk to the kitchen to start a pot of coffee. With her I know I won't be able to get back to sleep, not that I've been sleeping much anyway, and if I'm going to be up at God knows what time it is, I need caffeine.

"Wow, Mom and Dad really fucked you up." She slams the pot she is still carrying down onto the counter. "Do you know how stupid you sound right now?"

"Lots of people don't want to be married or to have kids, Lizzy."

"You're right, they don't, but I know that you are not one of those people, Mav."

"Maybe you don't know me."

"Oh, I know you, and I know that you not wanting to get married or to have kids has everything to do with our parents' fucked-up relationship and our mother abandoning you when you were just a little kid and nothing to do with you not actually wanting those things."

"You don't know anything."

"You don't think that I've had to deal with my own fucked-up emotions when it comes to family?" She shoves me out of the way so that she can take over making the coffee. "It took Landon forever to even convince me that he actually loved me and even longer for him to prove to me that he wasn't going to just get up and walk out the door one day." She looks up at me. "Even now there are days I talk myself into believing that I'm going to get home from work and he's going to be gone."

"Landon thinks you walk on water. He'd cut off his own arm before he ever hurt you like that."

"Yeah, well, from what Tanner tells me, this Jade chick feels the same way about you," she says, and pain slices through my chest because I know she's right. "I wish that I could have done a better job protecting you when we were kids, I wish that you never experienced the pain that you did, but I didn't have control over that." She shakes her head, looking sad.

"That's not on you."

"I know, but I hate that you don't see that you are deserving of love that is stable."

"It doesn't matter if I think that or not; it's already too late." I rest against the counter behind me and scrub my hands down my face. "Jade doesn't trust easily, and there's no way she'll believe me if I go crawling back now."

The truth is I've thought about telling Jade that I was being an idiot every minute of every single day since she held out her pinkie to me, but I've been a coward.

Over the years I convinced myself that I didn't want a wife or a child and told myself that shit over and over until I started to believe my own lie.

Then Tanner and Blake found women and started settling down, and slowly the truth started seeping in, which is why I pulled away from them a while back—not because they had what I wanted but only because I never thought I'd find a woman I could trust. I didn't think it was something in the cards for me.

Then Jade showed up and got under my skin, proving every day the kind of woman she is—loyal, loving, and a fighter—and then, being my own worst enemy, I pushed her away anyway because a woman can't leave if she never stays to begin with. I was stupid, beyond stupid, really.

"Do you love her?" my sister asks, pouring herself and me cups of coffee, and I don't even have to think about how I'm going to answer that question.

"Yes."

"And she wants a family and to be married?" she asks, and I nod.

"How do you feel when you think about her having those things with someone who is not you?" she asks, and my chest aches.

"Murderous," I tell her honestly, and she grins at me.

"Then, baby brother, you need to fight for her and prove to her that you're the man I know you are. Win your girl back."

~

"You know, I still want to kick you in the nuts," Margret grumbles from my side as I walk next to her down the sidewalk toward the coffee shop. "The only reason I haven't done that is because you look like shit, so I know you're already in pain."

"Thanks." I rub my hand down my cheek, wondering if I shouldn't have cleaned myself up a little before showing up here.

"You're welcome." She lets out a long breath. "So what is your grand plan to win Jade back?"

"I don't have a plan. I'm going to play it by ear."

"You're going to play it by ear?" she repeats, grabbing my arm to stop me. "Are you crazy? You broke her heart." Damn, there is that pain again. Who knew that loving someone meant that it was impossible to hurt them without feeling some kind of pain yourself.

"I'll figure it out when I see her."

"I just want to tell you that I don't think you figuring it out on the fly is a good idea." She falls back into step with me. "But she loves you, so maybe she'll be more forgiving for your lack of preparation than I am."

I smile for the first time in what feels like forever; then my heart starts to pound as we reach the coffee shop. I let out a breath while opening the door for Margret, allowing her to enter before me, and as soon as I step inside, I start to second-guess myself. The place is packed, so whatever happens between Jade and me will be witnessed by dozens of people, some of whom she will have to see every day regardless of how this turns out.

"It's too late to change your mind now." Margret pulls me farther inside.

"I'm not changing my mind," I tell her, then freeze when I spot Jade across the room talking to a man I don't recognize. As she smiles, I rub my chest, hating that I'm the cause of the dark circles under her eyes, which seem to be red rimmed.

"What are you doing here?" I turn to find Cybil coming toward me with a murderous look on her pretty face.

"He is winning back his girl." Margret steps between us, and I sidestep them as they talk quietly and make my way across the room. Like she knows I'm here, her eyes find mine, and a panicked expression replaces the smile she was wearing just moments ago. Between the music playing and the sound of people talking, I can't hear what she says to the man she is standing with, but I'm sure it's something polite like that she will be back, right before she takes off. Like a predator with its prey on the move, I follow her across the room, then out the front door to the sidewalk.

"Jade." I grab her arm, and she spins to face me with tears filling her eyes.

"Please don't do this." She holds up her hands between us. "Not tonight."

"It can't wait another night." I keep ahold of her, afraid that I will lose her if I let go. "I lied to you." I hold her gaze as my pulse thunders. "I can't be your friend."

"Good to know." She laughs without humor, trying to pull free.

"I can't be your friend because I'm in love with you, Jade," I tell her, and her lips part as she goes completely still. "I want all the things that

181

you want, to get married and have babies, but there is no one else out there I want to do those things with but you."

"Maverick."

"I know I fucked up, I know I hurt you, and I'm so fucking sorry about that, baby."

"You can't just suddenly feel differently about having a family, Maverick."

"You're the first woman I've ever trusted besides my sister, the only woman I've ever trusted with my heart. I'm sorry for not being open with you, and I know you might not believe what I'm telling you right now. But I promise you that I will prove to you every single day for the rest of my life that the same things you wished for on that star are the same things that I want with you."

"I never said I wanted to get married or have babies tomorrow."

"Then we'll have time before we take that step." I drop my forehead to rest against hers. "Please tell me that you forgive me."

"You hurt me." The sound of pain in her voice almost brings me to my knees, and worse, I know I did that. I caused that pain.

"I fucking hate knowing that I did that." I watch her eyes slide closed. "And I will do everything in my power to make sure that I never hurt you again. Just give me another shot."

"You have me, all of me. I didn't plan on falling in love with you, either, but somehow you stole my heart," she says quietly, and my chest aches for a different reason. Fuck, it feels good to know that part of her is mine.

"And if I tell you that I'm not ever giving it back?"

"Then I guess I have no choice but to trust you to take care of it," she says, and my throat gets tight.

"I'll always take care of it and you," I say, and she tips her head back so that her mouth touches mine. As we kiss, a loud roar goes up around us, and I realize that everyone from the party has come out to witness this moment.

"I think this calls for champagne," Cybil shouts, and I smile as Jade laughs. "Everyone, back inside. Let's give them a few minutes alone."

"You know," Margret says, coming over to us, "I didn't think your 'winging it' would pay off, and there were a few minutes there where I was sure you were going to go home without your girl, but that whole 'never giving her heart back' kind of redeemed you." She grins, then her expression softens. "I'm happy for you two."

"Thanks," Jade says quietly, and Margret smiles before heading back inside with Mason at her side.

Once the crowd has cleared, I look down at Jade, and she gets up on her tiptoes. "You love me?"

"More than anything." I kiss her softly, then rest my forehead against hers. "I just don't know how I got lucky enough for you to love me back."

"You're one of the best men I know, and as lucky as you think you are, I'm lucky that you love me." She pulls in a breath. "From now on, you have to talk to me. I know that's not really your thing, but I can't read your mind, so if this is going to work, we need to be able to communicate," she says just above a whisper, and I hate that she's scared that I'll do what I did again, but I get it.

"We have a lot to talk about. I have a lot I need to explain."

"When you're ready, I'm here."

"I got in my own way, baby. I realize that sounds like an excuse, but it's the truth. And even when I knew I should have told you that I lied, that I did want everything you did, I convinced myself that you wouldn't give me another shot after the shit you've gone through, so maybe it was better if I just tried to let you go."

"Us not being together would never be better for me." She cups my cheek, then leans up to touch her mouth to mine. "And just like you promised that you'll take care of my heart, I want you to know that I'll do the same with yours."

"I know you will." I hug her, then lean back and search her gaze, still shocked that she's here in my arms and that we are good. "We should head inside. It's cold, and this is your party."

"You're probably right, even though I feel like we should be heading home and celebrating us getting back together."

I grin at that and touch my mouth to hers quickly. "We will definitely be celebrating that when we get home." I lead her back into the shop, and as soon as we get inside, we notice that everyone is quiet and focused on Margret, who is crying, and Mason, the two of them standing in the middle of the room embracing.

"What happened?" I bark out, and Margret spins around toward us.

"I'm getting married." She holds up her left hand, and the ring on her finger glitters under the lights of the shop.

"Oh my God, congratulations," Jade says, sounding like she might cry.

"Thank you." Margret does a little jump right before Mason spins her around and bends her over his arm to kiss her.

I laugh at the two of them, not feeling envious like I have in the past, because I know one day a moment like that will happen between Jade and me.

And I look around at my friends, all holding on to their women as they watch the newly engaged couple, and know that I have what they do, which means I've got everything.

Epilogue

MAVERICK

Six months later

After walking into the living room, I stop at the edge of the couch, where Jade is lying with a book in her hands, reading, and shake my head. I never would have thought that Caz would be the kind of cat to accept human cuddles or another animal, especially one of the canine species, but I was wrong. Both Caz and Pebbles are attached to Jade. The two of them wait for her by the door when they hear her car pull up to the house, and if she's somewhere reading, they both cuddle together just to be close to her, like they are right now, curled into the curve of her waist. Their attachment is something I understand; I'm addicted to her, and even with all the time we get together, it never seems to be enough.

I never thought a love like this would be in the cards for me, but she proved that I was capable of so much more than I thought I was. With her I can clearly see my future, one that includes her at my side for the rest of our lives and our little ones running around us, driving us both crazy. That future is not only something I'm looking forward to but something I've started to crave for myself. Over the last six months, she's moved in to this house with me, and I thought that might be enough to hold me over for a while, but it's not, not even close.

"I can feel you staring at me." Her words bring me out of my thoughts, and I focus on her as she lowers her book to meet my gaze.

"Do you want to go on a ride with me up to the house to check the progress?" I ask, and her smile makes my chest warm, and the piece of metal in my pocket feels a million times heavier than it actually is.

"Of course I do." She carefully gets off the couch, leaving both Caz and Pebbles cuddled together. Two months ago the builders who are building our house put up the walls, and yesterday they added the tub in the master bath, a gift for her that she doesn't know about yet. "Let me just put on something a little warmer."

"While you do that, I'll pull the four-wheeler out," I tell her, wrapping my hand around her hip when she leans up on her tiptoes to kiss me.

"I'll meet you outside." She grins before she falls to her flat feet, and then she rushes to the bedroom, her hair down around her shoulders, her legs on display under my T-shirt, which she put on this morning after we got out of the shower.

Feeling anxious, I grab my keys off the counter in the kitchen, then head outside, where I pull the four-wheeler out from the shed and park it next to the front porch. When she comes outside a few minutes later, I place a helmet on her head, then make sure she's securely behind me before I take off up the road that now leads the way to the house that will one day be ours. As we get closer, the dark wood frame comes into view, and a sense of pride fills me. Growing up, I always wanted a place that was mine, a place that I wouldn't have to worry about moving from. And I might not have been able to get it then, but I have it for myself now, not only in the form of the house before me but also in the woman behind me. She's become my home, a place I feel safe, wanted, and loved.

"They put in the windows," she says behind me as I shut down the engine, her hands on my waist growing tight. "It's so beautiful already."

"It is. I just hope this weather holds so they can continue to work." I give her hands a squeeze before I help her off the four-wheeler, then remove her helmet before taking off mine. Last summer, the builders were able to get the foundation laid and the frame and siding put up, but then they had to put things on hold over the winter when it was too cold to work. Two months ago they got back on the job, and since then they've gotten a lot of work done, so with any luck the place will be ready to move in to by the end of summer this year.

"I know we're supposed to have some rain coming up, but with any luck they'll still be able to work inside," she says, leaning into me while we walk hand in hand into the house through the three-car garage. When we get inside, she lets me go to have a look around the combined kitchen and living room, which is better than I imagined it would be. The ceilings are tall, and there's a triangular window in the living room looking over the land below, as well as one large single-pane window in the kitchen above where the sink will be and sliding glass doors that will lead to the deck, which has yet to be built.

"Let's check the master." I lead her to the stairs, which are still unfinished, and walk behind her up to the second floor. When we reach the bedroom, I smile at the look of awe on her face. The view below is nice, but from up here we can see everything from the mountains to the town in the valley below.

"This is giving me princess vibes." She laughs, spinning to face me. "Do you love it?"

"I do." I walk to where she's standing, then take her hand and lead her into the bathroom. When we get there, the overly large claw-foot tub that they delivered today is in its place on the tiled floor in front of a large octagonal window.

"Maverick." She spins to face me and wraps her arms around my shoulders while resting her forehead on my chin. "I have a confession." She tips her head back to meet my gaze. "I knew about the tub." She shakes her head. "But I had no idea that it was going to look like this."

"You knew about it?"

"I saw where you had drawn it into the blueprints." She smiles at me. "But I honestly forgot about it until right now."

"Sneak." I smile, kissing her nose as she laughs.

"Sorry, but in all fairness you left them out in the open." She walks to the tub and climbs inside. I watch her for a moment, then go to her and urge her forward so that I can get in behind her. "Will you take baths with me?" she asks quietly, lacing her fingers with mine.

"You wet and naked is not something I'm going to miss out on." I smile as she laughs again, then wrap my arm around her upper chest when she leans back against me.

"This is nice." She turns her head so that she can look out the window, and I do the same, just enjoying the moment of quiet with her in a house that will someday be our home.

"This time next year we should be settled in here," I say softly, kissing the side of her head, then reach into the pocket of my jeans and pull out the ring I've had there since the guys told me earlier today that the bathtub was in place. Grasping her left hand, I hold it up in front of us and rub my fingers down her ring finger before sliding the platinum band with a large solitary diamond down over her knuckle. Her breath comes to a stop against my chest, and the silence that fills the space becomes almost deafening.

"Maverick," she breathes before turning around to face me, on her knees with her hands against my chest. "Are you sure about this?"

"Marrying you?" I cup her cheek, and she nods.

"I've never been more sure of anything in my life," I say, right before she falls against me, whispering "Yes" against my lips before she covers my mouth with hers.

JADE

Nine months later

Standing in a cream off-the-shoulder lace dress with a very pretty bouquet of wildflowers in my hands, I give Margret a reassuring smile, since she looks a little nervous. Two days ago our entire group of friends flew into Vegas, where Maverick, Tanner, Blake, and Mason got together and rented us a ridiculously huge fifteen-bedroom mansion just outside town with a pool, spa, gym, playroom, theater, and live-in chef. Since we got here, we've had the best time—we've gone to shows, gambled, and just spent time together, with all the kids and without them, since Everly's mom and Margret's parents flew out to help with all the babies. It's been a blast, but the real reason we are here is to witness Margret and Mason get married.

Months ago, when Margret came to me and asked if I'd be one of her bridesmaids, I of course said yes.

When Maverick and I were going through our thing, she was one of the people I leaned on and used for a sounding board, and since then I've considered her one of my closest friends—really, she, Cybil, and Everly each have a little piece of my soul. I never knew that I could be as happy as I am now, and part of that happiness is due to my friendship with each of them.

"Stop." I grab Margret's hands when she starts to fuss with my hair. "Today is going to be amazing. Relax," I tell her quietly.

I mean, really, she looks as gorgeous as always. Me, on the other hand, I feel awkward as heck in the dress that I'm wearing. I'm the only one wearing anything close to white due to my dress being lost some-where between Montana and Vegas, while she, Cybil, and Everly are all wearing dresses in varying shades of red.

The worst part is it's my fault. When we arrived and I realized what had happened with my bridesmaid dress, Margret assured me that she would get me something to wear, and a day later she hung a garment bag in my closet. I should have checked it then, but being busy and dis-tracted, I honestly forgot all about it. I let that bag hang there until this afternoon, when it was time to get dressed. Imagine my shock and hor-ror when I unzipped the garment bag and found the lace masterpiece that I have on now inside. Really, the dress is something that I would have chosen for myself if I were getting married, but I'm not getting married today, Margret is, so talk about awkward. Not that Margret seemed to care at all, which just goes to show how distracted she's been all day. I just know that when it comes time for photos, I'll make sure that I'm either hidden behind someone or out of the shot completely.

"I know. I'm just a little nervous," Margret admits.

"You have nothing to be nervous about." I give her hand a reassur-ing squeeze, and then we both turn when the door is opened.

"It's almost time," a woman who looks like Marilyn Monroe says, looking through our group.

"Thank you," Margret tells her, and then I turn my attention to Cybil when she comes to stand in front of me and takes both my hands.

"You know I love you, right?" she asks, and my brows drag together as I register the worried look on her face.

"Yeah, I know."

"And you know that I would never do anything unless I knew it was something you wanted but were worried about doing."

"What are you talking about?"

"Just promise that you'll love me no matter what happens in the next few minutes," she pleads, making me even more confused.

"You know I love you and nothing will change that." I shake my head at her, then frown when the door is opened and my dad steps into the room. "Dad?"

"Christ, Jade," Dad says gruffly as he walks toward me, and I look around at my friends, wondering if any of them can tell me what the heck is going on. But all of them are just watching me closely.

"What are you doing here? Where is Mom?"

"Right here," Mom says, stepping out from behind him, and I watch tears fill her eyes as she looks me over.

"What are you two doing here?" I ask my parents as they both hug me.

"We wouldn't miss your wedding day," Mom says with a laugh, confusing me even more.

"I'm not getting married today; Margret is."

"Surprise," Margret says, lifting her arms into the air.

"Surprise what?" I ask, and she pulls out a piece of paper from her bra and hands it over to me. After taking it from her, I unfold it, feeling my heart pound, then start to read the scribble writing that I know is Maverick's.

> Jade,
>
> I imagine you're wondering what is going on right now, so I'll tell you first that I'm waiting for you at the end of the aisle, where I hope to make you my wife. The truth is, I can't wait any longer to marry you, and this is the only way I could think to make that happen. Since we got engaged, you've avoided any talk of our wedding or babies, and I know that you've done it thinking that you're giving me the time I need, when the truth is there is nothing that would make me happier than marrying you.
>
> Over the last year and a half you've brought so much joy to my life. I wake up every day grateful that

you're at my side, and thankful for every moment I have with you. But more than anything I'm excited about our future, so I hope that you'll let your father walk you down and do me the honor of becoming my wife.

All my love,

Maverick

"I knew the note was too much. Now she's crying and her makeup is going to be a mess," I hear Margret grumble as I look between my dad and mom.

"I'm getting married."

"You are." Mom wraps her arms around me for a long moment before she transfers me to my father.

Closing my eyes, I rest the side of my head against his chest. Months ago, when Maverick drove me up the mountain to where our house was in the process of being built, I thought we were just going to check on the progress, so I was shocked when he took me to the bathroom where my claw-foot tub was, helped me inside, got in behind me in the empty tub, then slid a ring on my finger. When he asked me to marry him, I of course said yes.

Still, that didn't stop the little voice in the back of my head from warning me that it was too good to be true. I never doubted that he loved me or thought he was lying about wanting to marry me, but I did worry that he was rushing himself and asking me then only to make me happy. I wanted to give him time; I wanted to make sure that he was ready. That's why I've avoided the conversation anytime he's brought up starting to plan for our wedding or talk about babies. And I guess my guy is done waiting for me to figure out that, ever since we got back together, he's never been anything but honest about his wants and needs and is tired of waiting for me to get with the program.

"You tell me that this isn't something you want, and I'll get you out of here," my dad whispers close to my ear, then cups my jaw and forces me to meet his gaze. "That said, it would be a mistake. That man who is waiting out there for you loves you the way I know you deserve to be loved."

"I'm not going to run." I lean up on my toes so I can kiss his cheek, then look around for Cybil. When her eyes meet mine, I can see that she's a little unsure. "But I think I might need to fix my makeup."

"It's not that bad," she reassures me with a soft smile, and then I watch tears fill her eyes. "I'm so happy for you, and this secret has been so hard to keep."

"We'll talk about that later." I wrap my arms around her. "I love you."

"I love you too." She leans back to look at me, then transfers her gaze to Margret when she grabs my arm.

"As much as I love this moment, we don't have time. We need to get you fixed up so that you can get out there and marry your guy before he comes back here and drags you down the aisle."

"Right." I laugh as she leads me to a chair and forces me to sit.

As she fixes my makeup, my mind is spinning. Maybe I shouldn't be surprised by Maverick setting this all up. And as I search deep, I realize that I'm not even a little upset that he did. I love him, and he loves me; he's proved that over and over again. He said that I've brought joy to his life, but the truth is he's given that to me and so much more. With him I feel secure, loved, accepted, and appreciated. I don't know what I would do without him, or I do know, but it wouldn't be good. I know that I promised myself that I would be more cautious in my life after living so recklessly before him, but I now know that it's okay to jump without looking, because I know that he will be there to catch me. No matter what happens, he's got my back and I've got his. For better or for worse, he's mine and I'm his.

"All ready," Margret says, taking a step back from me, and I stand, then let out a breath. "You look beautiful."

"Thank you." I feel tears start to fill my eyes. "And since I know that Maverick dragged you into this, thank you for this too."

"What are friends for?" she asks with a smile, then adds: "But I hope when Mason and I get married next month, you'll still be one of my bridesmaids."

"Of course I will." I give her a tight hug, then smile at Everly when she gives me a thumbs-up.

I adjust my dress as I walk to my dad, and he gives me a proud smile as he takes my hand and places it in the crook of his arm. "Ready?" he asks, looking down at me.

"Yes." I give his arm a squeeze, then accept a kiss from my mom on the cheek before she opens the doors.

As the music starts to play, I feel my heart start to pound behind my rib cage, then wait for the girls to all walk out ahead of us before I force my feet to move. As I walk down the aisle, tears burn my throat. Not only are our closest friends and my parents here, but so is Maverick's sister, brother-in-law, and nephews. Four people I've fallen in love with over the last few months. I smile at his sister as I pass, and then the girls in front of me step onto the stage where Elvis is standing, allowing me to see the man waiting for me. Maverick is always beautiful, but today, with his longish hair pushed back away from his face, his skin sun kissed from the Nevada sun, and his eyes soft on me, he takes my breath away. When I reach the stage where Elvis is standing behind the guys, Maverick steps down to meet my dad, and the two of them share a few words that I can't hear over the whoosh of blood in my ears. Then, with a kiss to my cheek, my dad transfers my hand to Maverick's, and his eyes scan my face.

"Did you not think I'd show?" I ask him, just loud enough for him to hear, and he shakes his head.

"I would have tracked you down," he replies just as quietly, and I know he's telling the truth; if I hadn't shown, he would have found me, and maybe that shouldn't make my heart flutter, but it does. "Are you ready to marry me?"

"Absolutely." I smile as he helps me up the two steps to the stage. Standing in front of him in my dress with him in a tux that fits him like it was designed just for him, I can't help but feel like I'm in some kind of dream.

"You look beautiful, baby." His hands holding mine tighten ever so slightly.

"So do you." I smile when he chuckles.

"Are you two ready to get this show on the road?" Elvis asks, and we turn our attention to him and listen as he talks about the meaning of love and sharing a life with your partner. Even if the words are coming from an impersonator in Vegas, I can't help but think how perfect it all is and how I wouldn't change a thing. And when he tells Maverick that he can kiss the bride, I kiss my husband back, never feeling luckier for my string of bad luck, because if everything hadn't happened the way it had, I wouldn't have the man or the amazing life I have now.

MAVERICK

Three years later

Walking into my house from the back porch, where Tanner, Blake, Mason, and I have been hanging out watching the football game, I search for my wife but stop when small arms wrap around my legs.

"Dada." My son, Oliver, who is the perfect mixture of his mom and me, with dark hair like mine, his mom's and my complexion, and her hazel eyes, holds his arms out for me to pick him up.

"Hey, buddy." I kiss his soft little cheek as he wraps his arms around my neck. "Where is Mommy?" I ask him as Tanner, Blake, and Mason come inside behind me.

"I'm here." Jade walks toward me with her hands on her large round belly.

"You okay?" I kiss the side of her head when she leans into me and our son.

"Yeah, we were all in the bedroom using the ultrasound thing that Cybil brought over to check on the baby," she tells me as Everly, Margret, and Cybil come down the hall from the guest room.

"How's the baby?" I rub her belly, and she covers my hand with hers.

"Good, but Cybil is talking about making me go on a long walk to start labor." She rolls her eyes, and I smile.

"Don't worry," Margret says, coming to stand with us, her own belly half the size of Jade's. "I told her that it might be her baby growing in your wife, but she can't force her to have it early."

"Thanks, I appreciate that," I tell her, shaking my head.

Around the time that Jade was pregnant with Oliver, Cybil and Tanner admitted to Jade and me that they were not going to be able to have another child without the use of a surrogate and that they didn't think they would ever trust anyone enough to carry their child, so Claire would be it for them.

The night they talked to us about that, I found my wife out on the deck of our room crying, and after I calmed her down, she told me that she wanted to carry their child for them but wasn't sure that it was something I would be okay with. I can be honest in saying that it took me a good two weeks of researching, soul-searching, and talking to Jade to come around to her way of thinking.

Then, after a lot of conversations between the four of us, we agreed to move forward after Jade had had time to heal from Oliver's birth and settle into motherhood. It took two rounds of IVF for her to become pregnant, and any day now she will be giving birth to Cybil and Tanner's son. Something that I know the two of them are very much looking forward to.

"I'm just anxious to meet him already." Cybil rubs Jade's belly.

"I'm anxious to sleep through the night without my bladder being stomped on," Jade says, taking Oliver from me when he reaches for her.

"I forgot what that's like," Everly says.

Margret wraps her arm around her shoulders, asking, "When are you going to give me another niece or nephew?"

"In a few months," Blake answers before Everly can open her mouth, and we all laugh. "I'm serious." He shrugs.

"Wait, you're pregnant?" Margret asks, looking between her brother and his wife.

"I thought we were going to wait another week before we told everyone." Everly sighs as Blake wraps his arm around her waist.

"We already knew," Tanner says, and Everly shoots her husband a dirty look.

"You should know by now that Blake and the guys gossip like a bunch of schoolgirls," my wife says, tipping her head back to grin at me, and I touch my lips to hers, not even bothering calling her a liar, because she's right.

"I guess you're right." Everly lets out a breath. "Maybe we shouldn't let them spend so much time together."

"That will never happen," Cybil says, looking between us, and she's right. Blake, Tanner, and even Mason are my brothers, and I know it's the same for them. We've been through a lot together over the years, and now that we're all married with kids, we've just gotten closer. And the best part is knowing that our kids are going to grow up together. There will never be a time when they don't have people around who love them. And growing up like I did, I know that in this life there is nothing better than that. Family is love, acceptance, and showing up for each other. I always had that in my sister, and somehow I was lucky enough to find it with my wife and the people surrounding me right now.

About the Author

Aurora Rose Reynolds is a *New York Times* and *USA Today* bestselling author whose wildly popular series include the Until, Until Him, Until Her, Fluke My Life, Underground Kings, How to Catch an Alpha, and Shooting Stars series. Her writing career started in an attempt to get the outrageously alpha men who resided in her head to leave her alone and has blossomed into an opportunity to share her stories with readers all over the world.

For more information on Reynolds's latest releases or to connect with her, email her at aurararoser@gmail.com. And to order signed books, head to www.AuroraRoseReynolds.com.

Follow her on Instagram and Twitter (@Aurararoser) or on Facebook (@AuthorAuroraRoseReynolds).